POPPY OTT
AND THE GALLOPING SNAIL

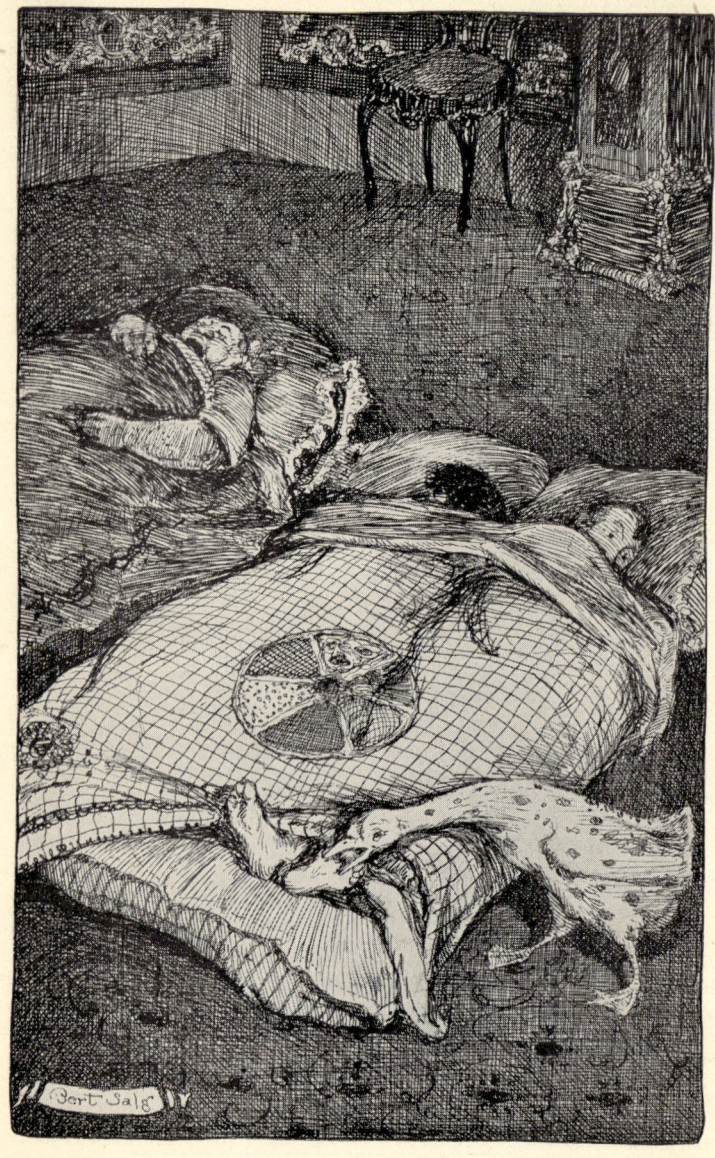

HE REACHED DOWN AND PINCHED MY BARE TOES.
Poppy Ott and the Galloping Snail. *Frontispiece* (*Page* 153)

POPPY OTT
AND THE
GALLOPING SNAIL

BY
LEO EDWARDS
AUTHOR OF
THE POPPY OTT BOOKS
THE JERRY TODD BOOKS

ILLUSTRATED BY
BERT SALG

GROSSET & DUNLAP
PUBLISHERS   NEW YORK

Made in the United States of America

COPYRIGHT 1927, BY
GROSSET & DUNLAP

TO
MY WIFE

CONTENTS

CHAPTER		PAGE
I	The Galloping Snail	1
II	A House of Mystery	11
III	The Spotted Gander	27
IV	Admiral Pepper	40
V	The Man in the Storm	48
VI	The "Ghost" in the Kitchen	59
VII	Lawyer Chew	70
VIII	All Aboard For Pardyville	83
IX	No Automobiles Allowed	90
X	Our Meeting With Goliath	100
XI	The Runaway	113
XII	Dr. Madden Comes Home	122
XIII	Poppy's Amazing Theory	132
XIV	Bit by a Grand Vizier	144
XV	A Scream in the Night	155
XVI	Getting Closer to the Secret	166
XVII	In Quarantine	179
XVIII	A Whispering Voice	187
XIX	The Diary in the Clock	198
XX	"Miss" Poppy Ott	210
XXI	Behind the Moon	222
XXII	On the Road Again	231

LEO EDWARDS' BOOKS

Here is a complete list of Leo Edwards'
published books:

THE JERRY TODD SERIES

JERRY TODD AND THE WHISPERING MUMMY
JERRY TODD AND THE ROSE-COLORED CAT
JERRY TODD AND THE OAK ISLAND TREASURE
JERRY TODD AND THE WALTZING HEN
JERRY TODD AND THE TALKING FROG
JERRY TODD AND THE PURRING EGG
JERRY TODD IN THE WHISPERING CAVE
JERRY TODD, PIRATE
JERRY TODD AND THE BOB-TAILED ELEPHANT
JERRY TODD, EDITOR-IN-GRIEF

THE POPPY OTT SERIES

POPPY OTT AND THE STUTTERING PARROT
POPPY OTT'S SEVEN-LEAGUE STILTS
POPPY OTT AND THE GALLOPING SNAIL
POPPY OTT'S PEDIGREED PICKLES
POPPY OTT AND THE FRECKLED GOLDFISH
POPPY OTT AND THE TITTERING TOTEM
POPPY OTT AND THE PRANCING PANCAKE

THE ANDY BLAKE SERIES

ANDY BLAKE
ANDY BLAKE'S COMET COASTER
ANDY BLAKE'S SECRET SERVICE
ANDY BLAKE AND THE POT OF GOLD

THE TRIGGER BERG SERIES

TRIGGER BERG AND THE TREASURE TREE
TRIGGER BERG AND HIS 700 MOUSE TRAPS

POPPY OTT
AND THE
GALLOPING SNAIL

CHAPTER I

THE GALLOPING SNAIL

ALL fagged out, I dragged myself wearily from the sun-baked concrete highway to the skinny shade of a thin-limbed, thirsty-looking bush.

"Under the spreading blacksmith tree the village chestnut sits," I crazily recited, kicking off my shoes to cool my blistered feet. Then I looked at my chum with begging eyes. "Get me some ice cream, Poppy. Quick, before I faint."

Boy, was I ever hot! I felt like a fried egg. But scorched as I was, inside and out, I could still sing a song.

To better introduce myself, I'll explain that my name is Jerry Todd. I live in Tutter, Illinois, which is the peachiest small town in the state. And the kids I run around with are the peachiest boy pals in the state, too, particularly Poppy Ott, the hero of this crazy story.

Poppy is a real guy, let me whisper to you. I never expect to have a chum whom I like any better than I like him. He's full of fun, just like his funny name, which he got from peddling pop corn. And *brains?* Say, when they were dishing out gray matter old Poppy got served at both ends of the line. I'll tell the world. If you want to know how smart he is, just read POPPY OTT'S SEVEN-LEAGUE STILTS. Starting with nothing except an idea, we ended up, under his clever leadership, with a factory full of stilt-manufacturing machinery and money in the bank. That's Poppy for you. Every time. A lot of his ideas are pretty big for a boy, but he makes them work. Of course, as he warmly admits, I was a big help to him in putting the new stilt business on its feet and teaching it to stand alone. But his loyal praise doesn't puff me up. For I know who did the most of the headwork.

With Poppy's pa doing the general-manager stuff in the new factory, my chum and I had merrily set forth on a hitch-hike as a sort of vacation. This, too, was Poppy's idea. A hitch-hike, as every kid knows, is a sort of free automobile tour. You start walking down the concrete in the direction you want to go, and when a motor car to your liking comes alone you wigwag the driver to stop and give you a lift. Sometimes you get it and sometimes you don't.

THE GALLOPING SNAIL 3

But if you limp a little bit, and act tired, that helps.

Poppy, of course, was all hip-hip-hurray over his hitch-hike idea. That's his way. Our most violent exercise, he spread around, seeing nothing but joy and sugar buns ahead, would be lifting our travel-weary frames into soft-cushioned Cadillacs and Packards. Once comfortably seated, we would glide along swiftly and inexpensively. No gasoline bills to pay. No new tires to buy. Everything free, including the scenery. Some automobiles would carry us ten miles, others would carry us a hundred miles. "We might even average around three hundred miles a day," was some more of his line, "and still have time each night to stop at a farmhouse and do chores for our supper and breakfast." If we slept in the farmer's barn, that would be free, too. Our trip would cost us scarcely anything, though it would be wise, the leader tacked on at the tail end, to carry twenty dollars in small bills for emergencies.

I fell for the scheme, of course. For Poppy never has any trouble getting me to do what he wants me to do. Not that I haven't a mind of my own. But I've found out that in going along with him I usually learn something worth while, and have a whale of a lot of fun doing it, too.

Having won our parents' consent to the trip, we had set forth that morning in high feather. But in poor luck we now were held up on a closed road, though why the road had been suddenly shut off was a mystery to us.

With a final look up and down the long stretch of concrete, Poppy came over to where I was and dropped down beside me in the hot sand.

"Still not a sign of a car," says he.

"Not even a flivver, huh?" I suffered with him.

"I can't understand it," says he, puzzled. "We saw a few cars after we left Pardyville. But the road's completely empty now, and has been for hours."

I saw a chance to have some fun with him.

"'And our most violent exercise,'" I quoted glibly, "'will be lifting our travel-weary frames into soft-cushioned cattle racks and pant hards.' Say, Poppy," I grinned, "was that last cattle rack we rode in a four-legged wheelbarrow or another gnash?"

"You won't feel so funny," came the laugh, "if you have to go to bed to-night without your supper."

"Bed?" says I, looking around at the sun-baked scenery. It was a beautiful country, all right—for sand burs and grasshoppers! "Where's the bed?" I yawned. "Lead me to it."

"This sand knoll may be the only bed you'll get. For there isn't a farmhouse in sight."

I got my eyes on something.

"The Hotel Emporia for me, kid," I laughed, pointing to a billboard beside the highway. "'One hundred comfortable rooms,'" I read, "'each with bath and running ice water. Delectable chicken dinners. Sun-room cafeteria. Inexpensive garage in connection.' Who could ask for more?" I wound up.

"Jerry, don't you ever run down?"

"Hey!" I yipped, straightening. "What do you think I am?—a clock?"

"Yah," came the quick grin, "a *cuckoo* clock."

"It took real brains to think up that one, kid. You win."

"It's a cinch," the leader then went on, "that they aren't letting any cars into this road. For we haven't seen an automobile since three o'clock. And it's after six now."

"Supper time, huh?"

"Yes, supper time, but no supper. Shall we walk back to Pardyville, Jerry?"

"How would that help us?"

"The automobiles must detour from there."

"First let us sleuth the road map," I suggested, "and find out where we are."

"Here's Pardyville," Poppy presently pointed out.

"We must be near New Zion," says I, squinting at the map. "See? Here's a river running east and west, with a concrete road on each side—C. H. O. and C. H. P."

"County Highway 'O' and County Highway 'P,'" Poppy explained.

"We must be on C. H. O."

"That's what the map says."

"Come Here Often," I made up of the three capital letters, looking around at the Sahara sandscape. "Yes, I will—not!"

"I should imagine," came thoughtfully, as the leader studied the map, "that a better scheme than going back will be to cross the river at New Zion and pick up the other road. For both roads lead into Sandy Ridge. And that's our next regular town."

"How far have we come?" I inquired.

The leader got out his "log" book.

"About sixty-two miles."

"What!" I squeaked. "Has it taken us all day to cover sixty-two miles?"

"Here's the dope: The first automobile carried us twelve miles. The next one kissed a telephone pole before it had gone a mile. The third one got on the wrong road and we lost seven miles. The fourth one—"

I let out a yip.

"The end of a perfectless day!" I sang noisily. "And you were the bird," I threw at him, "who said

THE GALLOPING SNAIL 7

that some automobiles would carry us a hundred miles at a jump. Poppy! Poppy! I believed in you, and now my sugar is salt."

"I guess I put it pretty strong," says he, with a sheepish look.

"I guess you did. Sixty-two miles! Hold my head, I'm dizzy."

"Anyway," he added, "you can't blame me because they suddenly closed this road."

"I suppose not," I let up on him. "But just the same I feel like a victim of circumstances, as the tomcat said when it sat down on the fly paper."

We got up then. And taking to the concrete again, we kept our ears sharpened for the sound of an automobile, for it didn't seem possible to us that the fine highway could much longer remain closed. But all we heard in the desolate strip of country was the rasping applause of happy-go-lucky crickets and the occasional bagpipe notes of a long-winded, hard-working locust. The waste land was an irregular checkerboard of sand ridges and clumps of unhappy-looking scrub trees. Men who jerked plows around for a living certainly had saved themselves a lot of grief and hardship by not stopping here. There wasn't a sign of a fence, which showed in itself that the land wasn't any good. Still, I concluded, it must belong to some one.

Weary from watching us all day, and messing up our faces with sweat, the sun, on its way to bed, was fast sliding out of the sky in the west. From a sizzling white moth ball it had changed itself into a big orange. The air was cooler now, but the concrete under our dragging feet seemed hotter than ever. It was like walking on hot stove lids.

It was Poppy's idea that the small town of New Zion, where we were going to cross the river, was just ahead of us, to the left, on a side road running north and south, between C. H. O. (where we were) and C. H. P. (where we wanted to be). But as we trudged along the hard roadway no sign of church steeples or shapely water towers came into sight. I was about to let go in weak-kneed despair, when suddenly the sound of an automobile cut the road silence behind us.

"Hot dog!" I cried, with new pep. "The road's open! We won't have to walk now."

But instead of a string of cars coming toward us from the direction of Pardyville, we could make out just one moving shape. It was far down the sloping road. Nor was the solitary car speeding toward us, though from the noise it was making, and the smoke, you could have imagined that it was scorching along at double the law's limit.

After an hour or two, more or less, the slow-moving,

smoking car got close enough for us to see that it was a roadster without a top. Maybe at one time it had been a fairly good-looking car. But that was years and years ago. In its old age it had gotten a broken back, which left the front and rear ends tipped up like the head and tail of a canoe. The sides were open—there were no doors—which in itself stamped the car as a relic. The windshield had long ago shimmied itself to pieces, though the brass frame that once had held the glass was still there. All four wheels toed out, like the wheels of Dad's brickyard dump cart, and one front fender was gone.

There was an old man in the car—a queer-looking old man, sort of stooped and thin-faced. He was hanging to the steering wheel for dear life. I waved to him to stop, but he didn't seem to see us at all, so deep was he in his driving job.

The crazy car having passed us, the noisiest piece of junk that I ever had seen on the road, I untangled myself from its smoky tail to find Poppy laughing his head off.

"The Galloping Snail!" he yipped, having read the name that was printed on the back of the car. "It sure is a 'Galloping Snail,' all right. Why didn't you jump in, Jerry?—you've been yelling for a ride."

"I didn't want to cheat the goose out of its seat," I laughed.

"Goose?" says the other, looking at me.

"Didn't you see the goose on the seat?"

"Who do you mean?—the old man?"

"No, a real goose."

"I guess it was a pair of geese," laughed Poppy, thinking of the queer driver.

Sometimes a fellow gets a hunch about things that he's heading into. But we had no hunch that we'd ever see that old car again, much less get mixed up in a crazy, shivery adventure with its queer driver and his equally queer gander—for it was a gander that I had seen, as we learned later on, and not a goose.

A spotted gander! Did you ever hear of one? No? Well, you're going to hear about one pretty soon.

CHAPTER II

A HOUSE OF MYSTERY

As though to completely take the joy out of life for us, no other cars came along, as we had expected they would. The sway-backed roadster with the crazy name and queer-looking driver seemed to have the whole highway to itself. And that was strange, we thought, puzzled.

Why had the road been closed to all the cars except this one? Or, to put it another way, if the road had been closed to the general traffic, for certain reasons, how had the one car gotten permission to come through?

It was dusk now. And as though cheered up by the cooler air of early nightfall, the crickets and locusts were tuning it up to beat the cars. Or maybe, was my crazy thought, they were hooting at us in derision as we passed. I could imagine, as we trudged along, hungry and fagged-out, that we looked not unlike some rare piece of junk that the cat had dragged in. I know I felt that way.

Once or twice we caught sight of a scuttling rabbit. And now that the bushes beside the hard road were lost in creeping shadows, I began to pick out moving eyes. Hunks of green glass set close together.

Poppy had joked with me about putting in the night here, though at the time neither of us had thought that we might in all fact have to do that very thing. But now the outlook was against us. We seemed to be a million miles from nowhere. Did snakes and sand lizards, I wondered, have green eyes? Br-r-r-r! If it came about, to our further grief, that we had no other choice than to stick it out all night in the open, it was my clever little decision to roost in a tree—that and nothing else but. I wasn't so well supplied with spare legs and arms that I cared to run the chance of having one chawed off and hurriedly digested by some green-eyed monster while I snoozed on a bed of sand burs. I guess not.

Certainly, I checked up on the day's adventures, so different from our dreams, a fellow's fortunes were easily turned upsidedown. Only that morning we had set forth on our trip with lilting hearts, as the saying is. Everything was sunshine and chocolate drops. But were we lilting now? Not so you could notice it. I had the beaten feeling, as I dragged myself along, that I had lilted my last lilt.

"Poppy," I suffered, feeling that it was time for some more nonsense, "if the worst comes to the worst, and I go down first, you can have my jigsaw

THE GALLOPING SNAIL 13

and football shoes—only the jigsaw needs a new leather belt."

"Merrily we roll along, roll along, roll along," the other sang, to cheer me up.

"Say, Poppy," I breathed, clinging to his arm, my eyes far away, "what is heaven like?"

"Be yourself, kid," he shoved at me. "You aren't Little Eva."

"I wish now that I had taken lessons on a harp," I tremoloed, "instead of a shoehorn. If only we could look ahead and know what the Fates have in store for us. Eh, kid?"

"Jerry," came warmly, as the leader slipped an arm around me, "you're a regular little sunbeam. For no matter how hard we get bumped, your stock of silly gab never dries up. I don't know how I ever could get along without you. Certainly, it wouldn't be the same old world."

Well, that was pretty nice of him, I thought. I appreciated the hug, too!

"If you want to," I puckered up, looking at him with my soul in my eyes, "you can kiss your little sunbeam . . once."

"Go on!" he shoved.

I was about to unhinge some more of my crazy gab, when all of a sudden the leader gave a whoop and scooted down the road.

"Here's a signboard, Jerry. 'New Zion ten miles,'" he read.

"Ten miles!" I groaned.

"We can make it."

"But look at the road!" I wailed. "It's nothing but sand. We'll slip back faster than we can go ahead."

"Then we'll walk backwards," came the quick grin.

"Ten miles!" I suffered anew. "It's no use, Poppy," I waggled weakly, as a sort of climax to my little act. "I'm done for. Remember, kid, the jigsaw's yours. And you'll find my book of patterns and seven new blades under the dog house. Good-by, Poppy. You meant well in bringing me here. But you didn't know, old pal. So I forgive you. And if you can't make the jigsaw saw ask Dad to help you, for he's almost as clever at sawing hunks out of his finger tips as I am."

"I'll 'jigsaw' you in the seat of the pants if you don't come on and shut up," he told me.

Seesawing together, the moon had been lifted into sight by the sinking sun. And now we could trace the winding course of the sandy road leading to New Zion. As I have hinted in an earlier paragraph, it was *some* road. Sand to the right of us, sand to the left of us and sand in front of us, as Lord Tennyson would have written it in poetry. But as I trudged along beside the leader I tried to grin and bear it.

"A light, Jerry!" he suddenly yipped. "There's a farmhouse up ahead of us. We're saved now, old kid."

There was indeed a house up ahead of us, on the right-hand side of the road. We could see it in the moonlight. But as we hurried toward it, in livelier spirits, I couldn't make myself believe that it was a farmhouse. Certainly, it was no ordinary farmhouse. For it was much too showy. I could count three stories and an attic. It was a stone house, too. And even if it had been built years and years ago, when labor and plaster were peddled around at bargain rates, I could not doubt that it had cost a fortune.

Who had been crazy enough, I wondered, curious over the unusual place, to build a house like this at the very end of the world? It didn't fit into the waste landscape at all. Still, was my contented thought, the better the house the better the meal. It ought to work out that way. So we really were in luck to strike a place like this instead of a shack, which would have better matched the country.

Not only was the house itself built of stone, but it was inclosed by a stone wall at least three feet high. Where the private road turned in, smoothly graveled, the wall was lifted into a huge arched gateway. Looking in, I thought curious-like of the magic palace that the genii had built for Aladdin.

"Is it real?" I asked Poppy's opinion, wondering if it would be safe for us to go in. "Or is it a mirage, as you read about in stories of people crossing the desert?"

"Tell me what you see," laughed the other, as puzzled over the unusual place as I was, "and I'll tell you what I see."

"A beautiful three-story stone house," I checked off, "with fancy jiggers all over it, to make it showy, and a stone wall in front, with a big gateway, like a cemetery."

"That's exactly what I see, too. So I guess it's real enough. But it beats me," the puzzled leader concluded, matching my thoughts, "to find a place like this in a country where there aren't even farmhouses."

Leg weary and hollow under our belts, it had been our intention to buy a meal here, late as it was, and if possible rent a bed for the night. Certainly, done up as we were from our first unsatisfactory day on the road, it was all right for us to draw on our emergency fund. The next night, when we were on the other road where the automobiles were, and playing in luck again, we would try working for our supper and breakfast, as we had planned on doing. But not to-night.

THE GALLOPING SNAIL 17

It struck me, though, as I stood there looking at the peculiar house, that this was no place to buy a meal. If we were admitted into the house at all it would be without pay. For only a very wealthy man could have built a place like this. And what would a dollar or two of our money mean to him?

Still, unless we wanted the people to think that we were tramps, it would be better for us to offer to pay for our supper, I told Poppy, than to ask for it. So of this determination we turned in through the big gate and mounted the front steps.

The door that we came to was set in a framework of glass, in the old colonial way, and taking a squint inside, I saw a long, wide, dimly-lit hall, the walls and ceiling of which were fixed up with fancy dark wood panels. It was a swell house, all right, as swell on the inside, with its beautiful walls and old furniture, as it was on the outside. And more than ever I wondered at its being here. It must have a queer history, I told myself.

"Clang!" went the old-fashioned knocker. And I stepped back now, out of sight, for a small, quick-footed woman of considerable age had come briskly into sight, carrying a hand lamp. I saw her set the lamp on a small table close to the door. In her blue and white kitchen apron, she didn't look very high-toned, like the big house, yet, to that point, I liked her best the way she was. She had a sort of motherly look. Her gray hair was combed tight to her head, which she carried very straight on her shoulders, and even before I got a close look at her I knew that her eyes were gray, too. I was to learn soon that they were very bright eyes, sparkling as she talked— and could she *talk!* Oh, boy!

The door was opened without hesitation. Yet at sight of us the woman seemed to be startled, even disappointed. She was looking for some one else, I figured.

"It's just two boys," Poppy spoke up quickly, noticing that the older one was trying to look over our shoulders. "We haven't had any supper. And seeing your light, as we were hoofing it for New Zion, we wondered if you wouldn't be kind enough to sell us something to eat."

"Laws-a-me!" cried the little old woman, with a nervous, excited gesture. "If you've got money, keep it. You don't have to pay for a meal in *this* house, not while *I'm* here, though how long I'll be here I can't say."

"That's fine," says Poppy in good manners. "But we don't want to be cheap about it."

"Samantha Ann *Danver* Doane is my name," the woman ran on, "*Danver* being my maiden name, and a name I'm justly proud of, I want you to know.

THE GALLOPING SNAIL 19

While it probably isn't anything to boast of, and certainly nothing to be ashamed of, I'll confess to you, as I have to other people, it being my nature to be frank and open, that I'm only a poor relation of the man who built this house and lived in it until his sudden death, the ninth of last August. So now you know who I am, and you understand what I mean when I say I don't know how long I'll be here. . . Who did you say you were?"

Poppy gave our names and explained about the closed highway. All the time he was talking the woman talked, too. It was kind of funny. But I kept a straight face. For even if old people are queer, you can't laugh at them to their face. I guess not. Mother and Dad would jerk me out of my skin if I ever did a trick like that.

"When you first knocked," the woman ran on, and I was getting wise to her lively eyes now, "I thought it was Miss Ruth. 'There,' says I to myself, as I dropped my work in the kitchen, 'it would be just like that dear jolly girl to call me to the door and then jump into my arms.' While I am a poor relation of the Danvers, as I say, I want you to know that I'm very proud of my stock, and consequently Miss Ruth is very dear to me, though I don't like her mother, and never did. The proud piece! But, laws-a-me, Miss Ruth is the *dearest* girl, just about the age of you boys, and just like her pa and her grandpa, too."

Talk like that takes a lot of air. But in stopping to get her wind, the little old lady didn't waste any time.

"*He* was the commonest and kindest man I ever knew in all my life, with all of his great wealth—meaning Mr. Corbin Danver, who built this mammoth house and died here—and how his son, Harold, could have quarreled with him, and let the quarrel stand to the separation of the two branches of the family, is more than *I* can figure out. But a lot of queer things happen in this world—and in the best of families, our own unexcepted."

"Yes, indeed," says Poppy, feeling, I guess, that to be polite he ought to say something.

The woman then switched her thoughts to us and smiled as though she had seen worse-looking guys.

"As I say, I didn't expect to find two *boys* when I opened the door, but you are none the less welcome, if that is in good form as coming from a poor relation. And you're hungry, you say! Well, just come with me to the kitchen and I'll see what I can find for you. I haven't had supper myself, figuring I'd wait until Pa and Miss Ruth got here, so I may take a bite with you for company's sake, for Pa may not get here for another hour. *Such* an old car as we have!

THE GALLOPING SNAIL

But it's all we can afford. You never know what is liable to happen to it when you start out. A wheel ran off the day we came here, which was a week ago yesterday. Oh, dear! It's awful to be poor. I sometimes wonder how it would seem to be a *rich* relation for once instead of a *poor* relation. . . Do you like cold meat sandwiches? Or shall I fry some potatoes?"

"Don't go to any bother," Poppy told her quickly. "For anything in the way of grub is good enough for us."

Having followed the woman to the kitchen, we now watched her, grinning at each other, while she worked and talked. Her hands and tongue moved together, though for the most part what she said passed over our heads. She kept referring to "Miss Ruth" and "Pa." "Miss Ruth's ma," we learned, had been a *Hardy* before her marriage into the *Danver* family. And considering her stock she was acting much too big for her shoes—whatever that was. But "Miss Ruth's pa" was a gentleman of *real* stock—a *Danver*, if you please! And "Miss Ruth" herself was just like her pa and her grandpa.

What interested us more than the woman's chatter was the fine supper that she set out for us. Boy, did food ever taste so good to us! I'd be ashamed to tell you how many sandwiches we ate. But however much we stuffed ourselves, we didn't eat half enough to suit the little old lady, who, having talked all the time she was getting the "eats" ready, was still talking. Her one great ambition, it seemed to me, was to tell all she knew!

Once she left us, to see if "Pa and Miss Ruth" were coming. We heard her open the front door and go outside.

"She sure has a limber tongue," grinned Poppy, murdering his tenth sandwich. "But she's all right," he tacked on hastily, not wanting me to get a wrong idea of what he meant.

"What do you make out of her talk?" says I, looking around the big kitchen, which was as fine a kitchen as I ever had been in.

"As I understand it, she and 'Pa,' her husband, came here a week ago to open up this house, which had been closed since the funeral—whoever it was that died here."

"I got that part—it was Miss Ruth's grandfather, Mr. Corbin Danver. He was the man who built this place."

"But who is Miss Ruth?"

"Some girl who's coming here on a visit, I guess."

"'Pa' went to the train to meet her, huh?"

"That's the way I understand it."

Poppy laughed.

THE GALLOPING SNAIL 23

"Say, Jerry, I wonder if that wasn't 'Pa' in the old car."

"He was headed this way, all right."

"Still," the leader turned the thought around in his mind, "it couldn't have been him. For the man who passed us in the Galloping Snail could easily have gotten here ahead of us. Besides, he was alone."

"Don't forget about the goose," I grinned.

"A goose isn't a girl."

"A lady goose is," I joked, "when she's young."

"You're a goose yourself!"

The woman was nervous when she came back to the kitchen.

"Dear me!" she cried. "I'm beginning to worry about Pa. For it's almost ten o'clock. Do you suppose he's lost?"

"Doesn't he know the roads around here?" I inquired.

"*Him?* Pa is dumb, if I must admit it, as one who has lived with him for more than forty years. *He* isn't a Danver," came proudly, "it's *me* who is. *He's* a Doane, and the Doanes, from Cyril Doane down, are a thick-headed lot, though I hoped well for Pa when I married him. But it's a fact, *he* wouldn't know how to put on his shirt if I didn't yank him into it. However, he's a good husband in some ways. For one thing, he never talks back to me.

But it's *me* who has to do all the planning. His head might just as well be made of wood for all the use he makes of it. I never can depend on him. The other day I sent him to Neponset Corners for some *baking* powder and he ended up in Sandy Ridge where he bought *bug* powder. Powder! That was all he could keep in his mind at one time—he knew I had said *powder*—but could he think of *baking* powder?—no, *bug* powder! That's Pa for you. No wonder I worry about him when he's out of my sight. And I wish now that I hadn't trusted him to go to Pardyville alone."

"We came through Pardyville this afternoon," says Poppy, by way of conversation.

"Like as not," came the further worry, "he'll go to the wrong depot. Oh, dear! What wouldn't I give to hear one of his old tires blow up out in front —just to know that he was home safe and sound. Suppose something should happen to Miss Ruth!— and her coming here secretly. What would her ma say? I sometimes think she shouldn't have planned to come here without telling her ma. And to that point, *why* she wants to come here, so secret-like, is a mystery to *me*. But when I got her letter, asking me to come over with Pa to open the house, I didn't say 'no.' That was little enough for a body to do for one's rich relation, I thought—and you always get something for it. As I said to Pa last night, 'Pa, *why* is Miss Ruth so anxious to come here all of a sudden? What is her object? Kept away from her grandpa's funeral by her ma, who never got over the quarrel, is she anxious now to come here, on her way to boarding school, out of respect for the dead?' But you might as well talk to a hitching post as to talk to Pa. All *he* ever says is 'yes' and 'no,' and half the time he doesn't know enough to say that if I don't tell him to."

I was thinking to myself, sort of grinning-like, that maybe all "Pa" ever had a chance to say was "yes" and "no." But, of course, I kept shut on my thoughts. For I know my manners.

As we finished our supper, the droning voice of a clock came down the stairs. I began to count the slow strokes.

"Listen!" the woman breathed, and I saw that a quick change had come over her. She looked frightened—as though she expected something to rush in and grab her. ". . seven . . eight . . nine . . ten," she counted. There was a short deep silence. Then something slammed upstairs. "What is it?" she cried, looking back and forth at us.

"Sounded like a door," says Poppy.

"I know it's a door. And I suspect that it's the door of the chamber where Miss Ruth's grandpa died. But what makes it *slam?* And always when the clock strikes ten! It does that every night. As I told Pa the second time it happened, there's something queer going on in this house—something that neither he nor I can understand. Miss Ruth isn't coming here in a mere whim. She has a *reason.* Has she learned why her grandpa left her the keys of this house? Does she know what is in the will, which is to be read here Wednesday night? Certainly, when she gets here, and I expect her any minute now, I hope that she tells me the truth. For if there's anything I hate it's to be around people who have secrets. *Me?*—I never had a secret in all my life. I don't believe in secrets. And that is one reason why I set my foot down when Pa wanted to join the Masons. I wasn't going to have *him* know things that *I* didn't know."

Poppy was sitting beside the telephone. And when it suddenly jingled he jumped as though he had been shot.

"Laws-a-me!" cried the woman nervously. "I wonder what now?"

CHAPTER III

THE SPOTTED GANDER

THE ghost theory is bunk. Every big kid knows that. *Ghosts?* Pooh! Who could be crazy enough to believe in ghosts? That is what we say back and forth, the *big* kids I mean, when the sun is doing its dinner-time stuff, high in the sky, and the nearest cemetery is six miles away.

But what happens when a white cow makes goo-goo eyes at us over a moonlit cemetery fence? Oh, boy! How we can cut the dust then. The only kid who ever beat me in a race like that was Spider Whickleberry, and his legs are so long that he modestly uses his pa's white duck trousers for basketball pants. And even then the pants aren't any too long for him!

Me believe in ghosts? Well, I should sa-ay not! But, to own up, what was the big thought in my mind right now? *Ghosts*, and nothing else but. Yes, sir, as crazy as it may seem to you, I actually believed in my excitement that there *was* a ghost in the upper part of the house. And what more likely than the ghost of the man who had died here?

At first sight the lonely house had struck me as

being queer. Not only in its unusual size, as it had towered in the moonlight, but in its desolate location, as well. Truly, had been my thought, no one but a queer-minded man could have wanted such a place.

Now I wondered if the dead man's secrets were living after him. It would seem so. Br-r-r-r! Certainly, I told myself, the elderly spook had a nice gentle way of letting us know that it was on the job! I wondered further if the door slamming, so sharp and businesslike, wasn't a gentle little hint for us to evaporate.

But the leader just laughed at me when I told him my thoughts. There was no such thing as ghosts, he argued. When people were dead they were dead— and once buried in the regular way that was the end of them so far as their earthly stunts were concerned.

"I'd sooner think," says he, "that it's tramps."

"Tramps?" says I.

"Sure thing. They've had the house to themselves since it was closed. See? And the door slamming is a trick of theirs to scare the old people away."

Mrs. Doane came away from the telephone with flashing eyes. It was Lawyer Chew of Neponset Corners, she told us, and we remembered then that Neponset Corners was the small town across the river from New Zion, on the other hard road where the automobiles were.

"He practically ordered me to leave here," the indignant talker galloped along, "but until Miss Ruth *herself* tells me to get out I'm going to stay right . . where . . I . . am. The idea of *him*, whose grandfather was jailed for horse stealing, and, worse, almost lynched, ordering a *Danver* around! My blood boils. Oh, the burden and humiliation of being a poor relation! But let him try to order Miss Ruth out of here and very probably she'll tell him what *I* hardly dared to tell him. For this is her house, though, of course, to a legal fine-point, she hasn't a deed to it *yet*. But everybody in the family knows that her grandpa left her the keys, and certainly, as I tell Pa, when we speculate on what *we* are likely to get, the old gentleman wouldn't have ordered the keys turned over to her when he was dead and gone if he didn't consider the place hers. Yet, even if she does inherit it—and we'll know the truth in a day or two, when the will is read—what good will she get out of it? For who besides a recluse like Corbin Danver would want to live in a place like this?"

"It certainly is lonely enough," says Poppy.

"Still," the woman added quickly, "*I* would gladly take it if it were given to *me*. Yes, indeed. But I'm not Miss Ruth. While *I* could live here if necessary, it would bore her to death, for she loves gayety and excitement. And what is there gay and exciting around *here?* Even the nearest town is a community of religious fanatics, who won't look at a talking machine or an automobile. Anything that isn't plain bread and butter and hard work is a worldly sin in their eyes."

"She means New Zion," Poppy nudged me.

"Of course, as I tell Pa, I haven't any hopes of getting this place, being no closer kin than a cousin. In fact, to that point, I haven't the slightest idea what I will get. I tried to pump Lawyer Chew the day of the funeral, for, of course, he knows what is in the will, being the family lawyer. But could I get anything out of *him?* No, indeed! Nor did any of the other relations, I venture to say. The seal of the will, he explained importantly—and if there's anything I hate next to secrecy it's over-importance!—was not to be broken for a year. I remember my feelings that day. In his lifetime Corbin Danver had been a deep man. Always thinking and scheming. I could tell you some very unusual stories about him. And knowing him so well, I realized that he had acted to a hidden purpose, both in giving his granddaughter the keys of his house and letting his will stand unread for a year. Yet, puzzle my brain as I would, I could think of no answer to the riddle. Nor did I, as I say, get

THE GALLOPING SNAIL 31

any help from Mr. Tight-mouth Chew! I was to have patience, he told me dryly. In due time I would learn if *my* name were mentioned in the will."

We were grinning now.

"Humph! I only hope, if Miss Ruth does inherit the bulk of the estate, as she has a right to do, that she gives that impudent-acting lawyer his walking papers. It rather surprised him, I think," and by a warmer look in her eyes, and a wag of her head, the talker showed satisfaction now, "to learn that the granddaughter had sent me here to open up the house for her. He hadn't much to say after I told him that. Maybe, though, I shouldn't have mentioned it. For Miss Ruth said I was to come here quietly. Yet how was I going to explain my presence here except by telling him the truth?"

"Say, Mrs. Doane," Poppy jumped in, when the long-distance talker put on the air brakes and stopped. "Jerry and I think we know what made that door slam."

The woman's jaw dropped, showing her false teeth, and for an instant she looked blank.

"The door!" she cried. Then she was herself again. "Laws-a-me!" and she started off at her usual snappy pace. "With Lawyer Chew trying to chase me out of here, I had forgotten all about the door."

"Had you thought of tramps, Mrs. Doane?"

"Tramps? I'd sooner think it was spooks," came bluntly.

"Atta-boy!" I yipped. "That's exactly what *I* thought, too."

"But, Mrs. Doane," argued old material mind, "there is no such thing as a real spook."

"No?" came quietly, and the peculiar dry smile that jumped into the woman's face, and out again, showed that she was holding something back. "Maybe," she added, unable, I guess, to longer keep her secret, "if you knew *everything* that has happened in this house since Pa and I came here you'd change your mind about spooks. I know *I* have. Doors slamming, footfalls in the dead of night, windows creaking in their slides, and every night that *queer smell* in the upper hall."

Poppy was staring now.

"Queer smell?" he used her words. "What do you mean?"

"When we first came here," the housekeeper ran on, only too glad of the chance, I guess, to tell her unusual story, "I thought I detected a peculiar smell in the house. Like drugs. But it seemed to go away when we let in fresh air. Then that night the door slammed. Pa and I had gone to bed. We got up, thinking that a window was open. But we could

THE GALLOPING SNAIL 33

find no open windows. And in the hall I noticed that peculiar smell again, only stronger. I asked Pa if he noticed it. 'A dead rat,' says he. 'No,' says I sharply, 'it isn't a dead rat—it's some kind of a drug.' Well, we went back to bed again, finding everything all right, as I say. Then the next night the door slammed again. And there in the hall was that same peculiar smell. The third night Pa and I watched. But first we went around and locked all the doors. Yet at ten o'clock we heard the sound again. And trying the doors, we found that the one leading into the master's chamber was unlocked."

"And you're sure you locked it?"

"I had told *Pa* to lock it, but, as I say, you're never sure of anything *he* does. The fourth night, though, *I* locked the door myself."

"And what happened?"

"We later found it wide open. And again that peculiar smell hung in the hall. Since then Pa and I have been locking ourselves in our room. Yet I never get to sleep until after ten o'clock. And always at the same hour, when the clock has struck ten, I hear the door slam. The last two nights we've heard other things, too—the creaking of windows, as I say, and even footfalls."

"Well, I'll be jiggered!" cried Poppy; then he got my eyes to see if I were as struck with excitement as he was.

"*Pa* always did believe in ghosts and the like," the little old woman ran on, determined to tell all she knew. "But *me*—it was a parcel of nonsense, I said. But now what can I say? I don't know how much of the situation you've grasped from my talk —and I guess, if the truth is told, I *do* talk an awful lot—still, I'm not ashamed of that trait, for it's characteristic of the women on our side of the house. There was my Aunt Samantha, for whom I was named. *She* was a real talker, to my notion. Laws-a-me! How I enjoyed my visits with her before she got paralysis of the jaw. As I say, I don't know how much of my talk you remember, rambling as it is, but I have tried to make you understand that *something queer* is going on in this house. You say it's tramps. I don't believe it. For listen to this," and the voice was mysteriously lowered. "When Corbin Danver died," came slowly, "*I* was the first blood relative to get here. I wanted to have a final look at him, before the others came, to see if the undertaker had removed the two ugly warts on his nose, as was proper, I thought, but Dr. Madden, who since has been in Europe, said 'no.' He had reasons, he declared, more important than warts, for keeping the casket closed. This, coming on top of the old gentleman's unusually sudden death, aroused my suspicions. And being of a determined nature—another Danver trait—I decided to see for myself. Nor did I even take Pa into my confidence. That night at twelve o'clock, with everybody else asleep, I crept downstairs . . . I was sickened for a moment by a strangling odor. . . You can see what I'm leading up to—every night since we have been here, at ten o'clock, the hour my relative died, that same smell seeps through the upper hall. A peculiar drug. I can't name it. And however much I have scolded Pa in the past about his silly belief in spirits, I now find myself wondering if the body of Corbin Danver, saturated with that drug, is indeed coming back in spirit form. And to what purpose? Has he some message for me?—some instructions? If so, why doesn't he come to me directly instead of slamming the door of his bedchamber night after night? And there is Miss Ruth. *Why* is she coming here secretly? Some one must have sent for her. But who? And now, in final, I have Lawyer Chew's ultimatum to get out of here promptly before the law puts me out. Oh," and the woman threw up her thin hands, a hopeless look taking hold of her tired face, "it seems to me that a hundred things have happened since I came here to unnerve and bewilder me. And how glad I am to have you boys to talk to, you can't imagine. I think I would go crazy if I had to be here alone very many hours."

Poppy got around so he could whisper to me.

"Do you believe her story, Jerry?"

"Sure thing. Don't you?"

"She may be cuckoo."

"You're cuckoo!"

His eyes began to dance.

"Oh, boy, if only we could sleep in the room where the old man died! The 'ghost' would get the surprise of his life, huh, when we yanked his sheet off?"

"I don't like it," I told him. But I wasn't scared. No. Ready to stand by him, as a loyal chum should, what worried me, I guess, was the thought that I might not be gritty enough to do my part in some of the crazy situations that were sure to bob up if we started any of the "ghost-catching" business. For "ghost-catching," let me tell you, even when the "ghost" is a man and not a real spook, is a mighty risky game, and nothing else but.

I'll never forget our first trip into the upper rooms of the big house. At every step I expected something to grab me. We went up the big front staircase, through all the rooms, one after another, where we looked under the beds and in the closets, then down the smaller back stairs. We went through the attic, too, finding all kinds of trash there.

Poppy's "tramp" theory exploded into thin air, we landed back in the kitchen at ten-thirty, having

THE GALLOPING SNAIL 37

used the small back staircase in coming down, as I say. Suddenly a fearful clatter came from the road.

"Listen!" cried the leader. Then he laughed. "Does it sound familiar to you, Jerry?"

"The Galloping Snail!" I yipped, scooting for the front door. Nor was I surprised to learn, after all, that the man we had seen on the road was the one this woman was watching for. Her talk about their "poor automobile" had put me wise, though it was a puzzle to me where the man had been all this time.

"It's Pa and Miss Ruth!" the woman cried, taking after us. "They've come at last."

Suddenly all sounds of the car ceased. And that was queer, we thought. Running down the moonlit graveled drive, we found the car on its side just outside the stone arch, where the driver, in poor work, had tried to swing out of the sandy ruts.

Thrown from the car, and getting his head cut, the old man was sort of staggering around like a groggy sailor. Then, before we could get to him, he keeled over in a dead faint.

"He's hurt!" the woman cried, and though, with her white face, she looked as though she were going to keel over herself, she kept up. "Help me, and we'll carry him into the house."

Poppy wiped away the blood.

"It isn't a deep cut, Mrs. Doane. He'll be all right in a minute or two."

It was then, I think, that the woman discovered that the car had brought only one passenger.

"Why!.." she cried in new alarm. "Where is Miss Ruth?"

The injured man began to mumble like one in a dream.

"Ma! Is that you, Ma?" and a fumbling hand felt around in the air.

"Pa, what have you done with Miss Ruth? Where is she?"

"Miss Ruth?" came vaguely.

"You went to the train to meet her. Where is she?"

"Miss Ruth?" the voice faltered, as its groggy owner, now sitting up, tried to explore his clogged mind for the truth. "Did—did I—I see Miss Ruth, Ma? I've plum furgot. It seems to me I did; an' then it seems to me I didn't. Now, Ma," came whiningly, like a little kid begging off, "please don't scold. You always scold. I guess I've furgot somethin' ag'in. I'm always furgittin' somethin' or other. But I'll go back an' git it, if you'll jest tell me what 'twas."

The woman's anger got the best of her sympathy.

"Ivor Doane! If you aren't the dumbest numskull I ever heard tell of." Then she seemed to go to pieces. "Oh, dear!" she wailed, turning to us for help. "Do you suppose he has lost Miss Ruth somewhere along the road? What shall I do? What shall I do?"

Suddenly I felt something nip the calf of my leg. Boy, did I ever jump. And when I looked down, there was the injured man's goose. It was wanting attention, I guess!

"The goose! The goose!" I yipped like a dumbbell.

But Poppy had better eyes than me.

"It isn't a goose, Jerry," he told me quickly. "It's a spotted gander."

CHAPTER IV

ADMIRAL PEPPER

THE mystery that hung over the big stone house, like a bat's shadow, was a strange tangle. We could see that, all right. And now, to help things along to even greater mystery, had come the disappearance of the granddaughter.

Was there, we wondered, some hidden tie-up between the girl's disappearance and the unusual gander? We looked to the old man for an answer to that, but he could tell us nothing. The more we questioned him, when we got him in the house, the dumber he acted. Had he seen the granddaughter in Pardyville? He didn't know—he *guessed* he had one minute, and the next minute he *guessed* he hadn't. Nor could he tell us where he had gotten the gander, which we had left on the front porch.

Another thing—the old man had passed us in his rickety car at six-thirty, headed for home. Yet we had beat him here by at least three hours. Where had he been in that three hours? When we asked him, he just stared at us. Where had he *been?* Why' he had *been* on the road headed for home, of course.

But we knew better. He had *been* some place else
. . to more mystery! Instead of turning to the left
at the sandy crossroad, where we had turned, he
had kept on down the concrete. But why? What
had taken him past the turn? Where had he been?
Finding it did no good to question him, we gave up,
hopeful that his head would clear up over night.

After the long day, with its ups and downs, Mrs.
Doane was done up, as her face showed. But it
would do her no good to go to bed, she told us, nodding
wearily. For how could she sleep with the awful
picture in her mind of the missing granddaughter
lying unconscious beside the deserted concrete highway?

"She could have jounced out of the car and Pa
never would have missed her. That's *him*. Oh,
at times I feel as though I could take him and shake
his pants off. He isn't foolish—don't deceive yourself on that point. He's just naturally *dumb*."

"Now, Ma—" came whiningly, as the blank-eyed
old man pottered around the kitchen, feeling of his
head as though it was some connected part of him
that he had just discovered.

"Keep still!" came the impatient command. "I'm
disgusted with you."

"Please, Ma—"

"And quit rattling your teeth," was the further

command. "For that's the way you chipped them last Christmas. And goodness knows we haven't any money to fool away on unnecessary dentist bills."

Poppy and I were grinning. Maybe it wasn't the best of manners, but we couldn't hold in.

"Oh, dear!" the woman went on in misery, sort of wringing her hands. "What wouldn't I give to know at this minute where Miss Ruth is. I'll forever feel guilty if any harm has befallen her through Pa's stupidity."

"Maybe," Poppy spoke up, "he missed her in Pardyville."

"But where did he get that gander? And why hasn't she followed him in a rented car?"

"The road's closed."

"But *he* got through. And there's the telephone. If Miss Ruth is in Pardyville, and can't get here except on the south road through Neponset Corners and New Zion, why doesn't she telephone? She might know I would worry until I *did* hear from her."

"Hot dog!" cried Poppy. "That's an idea. Why don't *you* telephone, Mrs. Doane? You can call up the Pardyville depot. See? And the garages, too. You ought to get track of the girl in that way."

The woman was too much worked up to use the telephone herself, so we did the job for her. But to no success. The night operator hadn't been at the

THE GALLOPING SNAIL 43

depot when the Chicago train came in—we'd have to talk with the day operator, he said. There was no one registered at either of the two hotels by the name of Miss Ruth Danver. Nor had any of the garages, or the taxicab company, been approached by a girl of that name, or for that matter any girl of any name, wanting to go into the country.

Our failure to get good news over the telephone completely upset the woman.

"What will Miss Ruth's ma say?" she cried. "Oh, dear! Oh, dear!"

Poppy remembered that the granddaughter had planned to come here on the sly.

"If I were you," he advised, "I'd wait a day or two before I telephoned to the mother. For you don't know as yet that anything really has happened to the girl. She may have hired a private car to drive her here."

"Sure thing," I put in, wanting to make the woman feel better. "We may hear her drive in any minute."

The old man was still pottering around the room.

"Ma, did I have my supper? I—I jest kain't remember. One minute it seems to me I *did*. An' the next minute it seems to me I *didn't*."

"Laws-a-me!" came kindly, showing that the woman didn't make a habit of jumping on the dumb old man all the time. "Of course you haven't had supper, Pa. And you must be pretty nearly starved, too. So come over here to the table right away. The boys ate all the sandwiches, but I guess I can make some more for you."

Poppy and I were sort of silent during the sandwich making, each doing stuff in his own mind. Nor did the woman talk as much as usual. Maybe her tongue was tired. I wondered if it wasn't!

"Jerry," the leader said at length, "do you know what we ought to do?"

"What?" says I, hoping that he would stick to schemes that weren't too blamed risky. Ghost-catching was my limit. Absolutely. Anything beyond that I'd balk at.

"If the girl isn't here by morning I think we ought to go to Pardyville and look her up. We've got time. And to tell the truth I'd like to talk with her and get at the bottom of this mystery."

"I'll let you be the hero and rescue the fair damsel in distress," I grinned, feeling kind of silly. "For you're the best lady killer of the two."

"I'm serious."

"A fellow *should* be serious," was my further nonsense, "when he gets ready to fall in love."

"You poor fish!"

I sort of brushed myself off.

THE GALLOPING SNAIL 45

"I wish now I'd worn my red necktie," I primped. "I might have stood a better chance."

"What you need is a *green* necktie," he fired at me.

"Jealousy!"

"Are you with me, Jerry?"

"Sure thing I'll stand up with you," I purposely tangled up his meaning. "What do you call it?—the best man, huh?"

"I mean, will you go back to Pardyville if I do?"

"Kid, I'd go to the North Pole, if you led the way—but that's a blamed co-old place, *I* think, for a honeymoon."

"Oh, you dumb-dora!" he gave up in despair.

"Say, Poppy," I snickered, "look at old Ivory Dome. He's scratching his sandwich and sprinkling pepper on his bald head."

"Ivory Dome!" the other laughed, thinking, I guess, that I was pretty clever. "Ivor Doane—Ivory Dome! That's a good one. He's an 'Ivory Dome,' all right."

Suddenly there was a wild volcanic eruption at the table. Over went the pitcher of water and the spoon holder. There was water and spoons all over the kitchen floor.

"For land's sake!" cried the housekeeper, grabbing a sandwich out of the air. "Pa, I ought to take a stick to you. Just look at my clean floor!"

"Ker-r-*choo!*" exploded the volcano anew. "Ker-r-CHOO!"

"Stop it!" as the table rocked more madly than ever. Then by quick work the housekeeper saved the sugar bowl.

"I—I—ker-r-*choo!* I kain't stop it—*KER-R-CHOO-O-O!*"

"He sprinkled pepper on his head instead of the sandwich," grinned Poppy.

"Laws-a-me! That isn't anything surprising for *him*. One time he put a bunion plaster on his jaw and cleaned his toes with the tooth brush."

Having lived through the eruption, the old man was staring now, as though the sneezing and its cause had jarred loose some corner of his memory.

"Pepper," came in a mumbling, unsteady voice. "Pepper. *Admiral Pepper*. That's it."

Admiral Pepper! What crazy thing was he talking about? It was our turn to stare now.

Suddenly there was a faint tap! . . tap! . . tap! . . on the outside kitchen door. And scared out of her wits, Mrs. Doane ran screaming into another room.

"Who is it?" says the leader, tiptoeing to the door, his right ear shoved out ahead to catch every possible sound.

Tap! . . tap! . . tap! . . That was the only answer.

THE GALLOPING SNAIL 47

Well, I don't mind telling you that this was another moment in my life when I didn't have to overwork my imagination to believe in ghosts. I guess not. The thing that was doing the tapping, I told myself, was a ghost, probably a long, lean, hungry-looking ghost with two or three hideous heads, and nothing else but.

Then, as though unlatched by some unseen hand, the door swung open. A gust of wind swept in. And in walked—not a three-headed ghost—but that blamed spotted gander!

"Why—why," fumbled the old man, acting sort of tickled as he got his eyes on the gander. "It's jest Mr. Pepper. I mean Mr. Salt an' Pepper. No, I mean—I mean—Now," came blankly, as the feeble brain got completely tangled up, "what *do* I mean, anyway?"

"I guess," supplied Poppy, staring at the flat-footed newcomer, "you mean *Admiral* Pepper."

"Admiral Pepper!" the wrinkled face cleared up. "That's it. That's it."

CHAPTER V

THE MAN IN THE STORM

ADMIRAL PEPPER! That was some fancy handle, I thought, for a gander. But I saw right off that it was no ordinary gander. So the name was all right.

White, like most ganders, though peculiarly marked with small purple spots, it was the biggest fowl of its kind that I ever had seen. Standing on its webbed feet, which reminded me of a pair of palm-leaf fans, its tonneau, as we used to call the rear end of an automobile, sort of dragged behind like an overloaded dump cart. Of course, like all big geese, it waddled when it walked. Yet it had dignity in its waddle. A fat king, you know, would waddle much more becomingly than a fat junk peddler! There was further dignity in the way it held its big head—carriage, I guess you'd call it. It seemed to have no fear of us. To the contrary, in its lordly possession of the house, it sort of acted as though we ought to consider ourselves lucky that we weren't boosted outside along with the other unimportant rubbish!

I've seen people act like that. Stuck-ups. They

sort of strut around as though they're the whole cheese, smell and all. The other human beings in the landscape aren't even presentable scenery. So my conclusion was that Admiral Pepper, as the saying is, belonged to the aristocracy—the gander-land aristocracy, if you please!

Unlike the ordinary barnyard variety of geese, this one didn't honk its horn at us, nor did it do any long-necked hissing stuff. Its dignity was too strong. And to that point, having already mentioned a king, can you imagine a ruler, on his grand entrance into the official throne room, yipping to his subjects to stand back and not get any shoe blacking on his long velvet train! Hardly! You see what I mean, I guess.

One time we had a rather strange adventure with a performing hen. I told about that in detail in another book, JERRY TODD AND THE WALTZING HEN. Now I wondered if the gander, like Isadora, the waltzing hen, hadn't been brought up for the most part, and to a purpose, in a circus. Plainly, it was a pet. It showed in its actions that it was used to living with people instead of birds of its kind. Moreover, it expected special attention, which further went to prove that whoever had owned it had been in the habit of making a big fuss over it. Could it do circus tricks? I wondered.

Recalling Isadora, the thought then jumped into my head that it would be wise for us, if the granddaughter didn't show up, to inquire in Pardyville if an animal show had stopped there recently. If so, that would sort of explain the old man's possession of the unusual bird. To some crazy purpose it could have followed him out of the show tent, or, to his discredit, he could have stolen it. Certainly, familiar as he was with its name, he must know where it came from. He had the stuff in his head to tell us. The trouble was his memory was like a locked door— he couldn't open it until he found the key.

Well, to pick up my story, we shut the kitchen door, convinced now that the wind had opened it. It was queer, of course, that the latch had slipped just when the gander wanted to come in. But that was nothing. Very probably the visitor, hearing us inside, had been waiting at the door for some time, hoping for a chance to get in. And wise to the growing wind and darkened moon, which meant a summer storm, it had done its tap! . . tap! . . tap! . . stuff, to get shelter, just when the wind was strong enough to spring the loose latch.

Taking a sort of shine to the unusual gander, with all of its stuck-up ways, Poppy and I would have made it comfortable for the night in the kitchen, if we had been boss. But the thought of keeping a

THE GALLOPING SNAIL 51

gander in the house, even though it was an unusual gander, and probably house broken, was too much for Mrs. Doane. You should have heard her explode when we suggested it!

"Laws-a-me!" she stiffly turned us down, getting a broom to drive the intruder away. "Why don't you think next of turning the house into a pigsty? If you're so deeply concerned over the gander's comfort, there's a barn out back. Certainly, it isn't going to roost *here*. Imagine what Corbin Danver would say, could he speak from the grave, to have his kitchen turned into a gander roost. Just *imagine!*"

The moon was gone now, as I say. The sky was black with tumbling storm clouds. And on the way to the barn, where we fastened the gander in for the night, Poppy and I used a flashlight. What a quick change, I thought, from early evening. The moon had been full of light then. Now the whole world was smothered under a heavy black blanket.

I don't mind summer storms as a rule. The lightning never scares me. For I have a sort of feeling that God makes the lightning. And certainly, with me taking up the Sunday-school collection week after week, and never hooking a penny, but cheerfully giving instead, He wouldn't want to jab the deadly lightning at me. That wouldn't be right. When you're good you expect to be used good. No, even if the lightning is close by, I have a sort of steady confidence that no harm will come to me. The thunder, of course, makes a fellow jump, especially if he's half asleep. But a few jumps more or less isn't anything. As for the rain, I love to hear it— when I'm in bed, I mean. Some rainy nights when it isn't too hot I sleep in the attic, just to hear the patter! patter! on the roof. Music like that brings out all the peace that there is inside of a fellow, I want to tell you.

But to-night I seemed sort of unprotected in the growing storm. I felt as though certain *black* scheming things that God's moonlight had kept away were creeping in to an evil purpose. Couple up a slashing, pounding storm with this mysterious house, I thought, and there was no telling what wasn't liable to happen.

Returning to the house, after taking care of the gander, we heard Mrs. Doane putting her thickheaded husband to bed on the second floor. Earlier in the evening she had pointed out a room for us— though not the room that Poppy had hoped for!— and as it was long past our own bedtime, as well as the old man's, we locked the lower doors and lighted our way up the back staircase with a small hand lamp.

Outside, the wind was swishing around the corners

THE GALLOPING SNAIL 53

of the house to beat the cars. And a giant, or so it seemed to me in crazy fancy, was slinging sand at the windows by the scoop full. Boy, was I ever glad now that I was inside, and not out there!

Pretty soon the rain came. Not an ordinary rain, but a sort of mixed up cyclone and cloudburst. It was *some* storm, let me tell you. I never hope to see a worse one. Looking down on the yard, in the lightning flashes, I could see a big lake. The sand had turned into water.

"Well," grinned Poppy, as he slid out of his clothes, "I wonder what the program is for to-night."

He was thinking about the ghost, of course.

"Maybe we ought to take turns staying awake," says I.

"Nix. We want the ghost to come. And it won't come if we aren't asleep."

"Just back up," I fired at him, fishing my nightie out of the little bag that held my truck—an extra shirt, tooth brush, and things like that—"if you think that little sugar plum is going to let old spooky foot catch him asleep."

"The ghost isn't going to catch *us*—we're going to catch *it*."

"'It' or 'him,' which?"

"It's a 'him,' all right. . . I wonder who it is."

Bang! went a bucket of water against the window.

"Some storm!" I cried.

"A *queer smell*,". mused Poppy, recalling the housekeeper's story, "footsteps in the dead of night, windows creaking in their slides." Then he laughed. "I hope that the spook, whoever he is, puts on the whole show to-night."

"Lock the door," says I, "and push the dresser in front of it."

"Cuckoo! We'd stand a fine chance of catching the ghost if we locked ourselves in. Do you suppose he's going to smash the house down to get at us?"

"Then we aren't going to lock the door?"

"Absolutely not."

"That being the case," I grinned, making a dive for the bed, "I know who's going to sleep next to the wall."

Settled cozily in bed, Poppy then began at the beginning of the mystery, as we understood it, and went over it step by step, the better, I guess, to sort of figure out what was liable to happen to us if we took a notion to work on it!

And listening, I became sort of fascinated. I thought of other mysteries that we had solved—the talking frog, the rose-colored cat, the Oak-Island treasure, the whispering mummy, the stuttering parrot. What a wonderful chance this was, I told

myself, all worked up, for a clever little Juvenile
Jupiter Detective to show his stuff.

First of all, in Poppy's check-up, came the strange
house itself. Why had it been built here? Or, to
put the question another way, what had been Mr.
Danver's hidden purpose in building it here—a fifty-
thousand-dollar mansion on a ten-cent farm? Was
it to be alone? Possibly. Then in his lifetime he
must have been a sort of recluse. It isn't hard for a
recluse to get kind of queer in his head, so we could
safely conclude that the dead house owner had been
queer. Therefore he was subject to doing queer
things—could even have planned things to happen
to a queer purpose after his death.

All right. That was that.

To go further, there had been a son, Harold Danver,
of whom we knew very little except that he had
quarreled with his father, nor had the quarrel been
patched up at the time of the younger one's death.
Married to a woman who was "much too big for her
shoes," to use the housekeeper's words, the son had
left a daughter named Ruth, or, as the housekeeper
had respectfully expressed it, "Miss Ruth." The
daughter-in-law with the big feet had kept up the
family quarrel, even telling the granddaughter that
she couldn't go to the funeral when the head of the
house died. At the death, which had been sudden—

and this hinted at mystery!—all of the relatives had flocked in, of whom none were more hopeful of getting a handful than "Ma" and "Pa." Disappointment!—the will wasn't to be read for a year. On this occasion "Ma" had gone snooping, to the awful discovery that the casket had a "queer" smell—a drug-store smell. Evidently after the funeral the house had been closed up and the keys sent to the granddaughter. Since then the better part of a year had passed. And now, when it was almost time to open and read the will, the granddaughter had made mysterious plans to have the house opened for her. She was to come quietly and secretly on the seventh of the month, which was two days before the time set for the reading of the will. Coming to the house at the granddaughter's secret request, "Ma" and "Pa" had found "queer smells," slamming doors, creaking windows, and the like.

We spread out the dope like this:

(1) Had Corbin Danver died naturally? Or if certain life secrets had something to do with his sudden death, what were those secrets? Was it possible for Poppy and I to get wise to them?

(2) Why had the grandfather given the granddaughter the keys of his home? Why did he want his will shut up for a year?

THE GALLOPING SNAIL 57

(3) Was the will going to be a big surprise to the relatives?

(4) Were certain people secretly posted on the will doing stuff ahead of time to make themselves safe when the will was read?—the granddaughter, for instance. (The "queer smell," door slamming, and so on, came in here.)

(5) What was the connection, if any, between the granddaughter's disappearance and the spotted gander? Where had "Pa" been during the earlier part of the evening?

(6) What was liable to happen to Poppy and I if hidden eyes caught on that we were trying to untangle the mystery, as we wanted to do, if the chance came our way?

Well, as I say, with the door wide open and so much "ghost" talk in my head, I had no idea of going to sleep. It didn't seem possible to me that I could drop off. Yet I did. And so did Poppy.

Suddenly I was lifted ten feet into the air by an old gee-whacker of a thunderclap. And when I came down to earth again, and realized where I was, maybe you think I didn't do some quick neck-stretching to see if there was anything white in the room with us. But we were safe.

Boy, was it ever pouring outside! I got up and went to the window. I don't know—maybe, half awake and half asleep as I was, I expected to see the bushes floating around. Or even the barn.

A hundred electric generators were sending out lightning flashes. One after another. So it was easy for me, and for Poppy, too, who stood beside me, to see the flooded world below.

Suddenly the other caught his breath. He had seen something!

"Jerry!" he pointed. "Look down there by that big bush. No, more to the right. What do you see?"

"A man," I breathed.

The leader then began to jerk on his clothes. And I knew without being told that he was going out in the storm to learn, if possible, who the spy was.

That's old Poppy for you! Every time! And do I ever love that kid for his wonderful grit. He's one pal in a million.

CHAPTER VI

THE "GHOST" IN THE KITCHEN

"Now," says Poppy, when he was dressed, "you wait here at the window. I'll go out the back way, taking the door key with me. And to play safe, I'll circle to the front road. You may not see me at first. But don't let that fuss you. Give me ten minutes and I'll be there."

I felt sort of calfy in the separation—as though he was giving me the soft end.

"Why can't I go, too?" says I, wanting to be as brave as he was. "Then you'll have me if you need me."

But he shook his head, laughing.

"You're the guy who lights up the old South Church tower," says he.

Every American kid knows that poem.

"And who are you?" I grinned, getting a slant on his scheme. "Paul Revere in a raincoat?"

"Bu-lieve me," came with another laugh, "it would be 'Paul Revere in a bathing suit,' if I had one. For I hate the thought of getting these clothes soaked. I guess, though, it can't be helped."

I hinted around then that a little lucid information about my "old-South-Church-tower" job wouldn't be out of place. So he got down to business.

"Here's the dope, Jerry: You're to watch that guy down there. If he moves to another bush, or toward the house, keep track of him. Then, as in the poem, twitch your flashlight *once* if he's still there, and *twice* if he's moved. Getting your signal, I'll let you spot me in the lightning and signal back with my cap. See?"

"I get you," I nodded, writing down the instructions in my mind.

"After that," came the further dope, "keep track of us both, and guide me. One flash up and down will mean that I'm 'cold,' two will mean that I'm 'warm,' and three will mean *danger*—scoot for your life. But keep a steady grip on yourself, old pal, and don't flash 'danger' unless there *is* danger. When I'm all through, I'll signal again with my cap. Then you can wait for me in the kitchen, where we'll dry my clothes."

Left alone, and kind of shaky, too, in the separation, I got my nose against the window, as the leader had said. I was careful, though, not to show myself any more than I could help. For I didn't want the spy to get hep to the fact that I was watching him, while he in turn watched the house.

THE GALLOPING SNAIL 61

Poppy had said to give him ten minutes. So I started counting off the seconds. When I came to sixty that meant a minute, and I crooked a finger. Pretty soon I had all ten fingers and thumbs crooked. So I got ready with my flashlight.

The man hadn't moved. That is, he was still behind the bush where we first had seen him. So I gave one flash. I did it in the dark, of course, though it wasn't dark very often, for the lightning, like an octopus, was swinging a hundred fiery tails.

Watching the road beyond the stone wall, I presently got sight of Poppy, a sort of skulking black spot in the continued storm. He was waving his cap, showing that my first signal had gotten to him all right. I was glad to see him. I felt safer in knowing that he was safe. Then, on the job, I gave him two quick up-and-down flashes, for the sharp-eyed spy, as though alarmed by the window signal, was heading for the road, and that, as I say, is where my chum was.

But pretty soon the man stopped short and sort of crouched behind another bush, of which a dozen or more were scattered, to a fancy plan, up and down the edges of the graveled drive. Poppy was inside the stone wall now. He was getting closer and closer to the spy, so I kept on with the two up-and-down flashes. The signals were working as slick as a button.

I thought how easily I could yank my chum out of danger—three twitches of my thumb, as it rested on the switch, and the trick would be done. He could scoot to cover before the man caught him. Easy.

And now comes a part of my story that I hate to write down. The recollection of it gives me cold shivers. Talk about trapped people turning gray-headed over night! The wonder to me is that my hair didn't turn *green*.

The flashlight suddenly went on the bum. There you are! You can see what a fix I was in, or, rather, what a fix Poppy was in. Getting no signals from me, he would think that everything was lovely. He'd keep on. And how was I going to warn him if the spy took after him?

Matches! As the thought jumped into my head, I ran to the dresser. But to no success. Then, sort of crazy, I began to go through my clothes, though I should have known that I would find no matches there—for what few matches we carried were in a waterproof case in Poppy's hip pocket. In dividing our truck he had taken the matches and I had taken the cake of soap.

I remembered then that there were matches galore in the kitchen. I had seen them in a little box near the stove. To get a handful wouldn't take more than

THE GALLOPING SNAIL 63

a minute or two. Hot dog, was my great joy. I could save old Poppy yet.

I was out of the room and down the hall like a streak. Nor did I miss a lamp, for by fits and jerks, as the lightning came and went, the hall, with its big end windows, was almost as bright as day.

Scooting along in my bare feet I made no more sound than a cat. Nor did I stir up any racket on the back stairs. Suddenly, though, as I came to the bend in the stairs, I stopped short. Talk about slamming on the *brakes!* Boy, I skidded seventeen feet with locked wheels. Smell the rubber. Phew! There was a light in the kitchen. A moving light. Its reflection on the wall ahead of me, where the stairs turned, is what had stopped me.

It wasn't Poppy. I knew that. As for Mrs. Doane and her cuckoo husband, they were in bed. Seemingly, I thought, with a queer feeling not easy to explain, I had tumbled into an entirely new part of the mystery!

Was it the ghost? If so, then the spy in the storm was a second party, of whom we knew nothing, for certainly, as my good sense pointed out, the man couldn't be in both places at once.

I suddenly was sort of suffocated under the weight of the growing mystery. It seemed so—so sort of *tremendous*. A spy outside, with the rain beating down on him (though evidently he didn't notice it or mind it) and a "ghost" inside! How many more people were there, I wondered, in the crazy hidden tangle? And whether they were working together, or against each other, what was their secret purpose? Property! That must be it. In his grave less than a full year, his will about to be read, greedy hands were already reaching out in the dark, in evil schemes, for the dead house-owner's property. That's the way it is when some rich men die. And Corbin Danver, the housekeeper had told us, had been a millionaire.

I don't think that it's any discredit to me that I sort of dropped Poppy out of my mind at this point. He was able to take care of himself, was my quick decision, seeing that I had other work to do. Not being dumb, he'd begin to wonder when the signals stopped. He'd go slow. And that would make him safe. In a pinch, he could take to long legs, and outside of Spider Whickleberry and myself, if there's anyone who can fan legs any faster than old Poppy, I don't know who it is, though usually he runs *at* things instead of away from them.

Yes, the leader was safe enough, I concluded. And to that point, he might even be safer than me! For here I was, not twenty feet from the ghost, and wanting to go on, to see who the "spook" was, there

STOOPED OVER, HE WAS DOING SOMETHING TO THE LOCK OF THE KITCHEN DOOR.

Poppy Ott and the Galloping Snail. *Page* 65

THE GALLOPING SNAIL 65

was no telling where I might end up. Instead of the leader getting laid out cold, it might be little dewdrop!

But here was my chance; I hung on doggedly. I wasn't going to back down. For how would Poppy feel toward me to learn that I had hid from the ghost in a closet? No, instead of backing up, the thing for me to do, I realized, getting out all my grit, was to go farther down the stairs, even around the bend. Then I could see into the kitchen.

So down I went, slowly you may be sure, and on tiptoe. I was at the bend now. Another step; two steps. I could see a man in a long white nightshirt—ghostly enough, all right! Stooped over, he was doing something to the lock of the kitchen door.

Well, if you must know the truth, I felt sort of weak as the "ghost" turned his face. For who do you think it was? Yah, you guessed it—nobody but old Ivory Dome himself!

As I say, the discovery sort of amazed and stunned me. And yet, I thought, my mind jumping back to the housekeeper's crazy story, who besides old Ivory Dome could better have played the "ghost" here? Dumb in his wife's eyes, the finest chance in the world had been given him to fool her. And he *had* fooled her, all right! More than that, he had fooled all of us. He let on that he didn't know where the granddaughter was. But he did. He knew the gander's secret, too. In fact he knew a hundred things in the mystery that his sharp-tongued wife never suspected, with all of her wonderful family smartness! *She* was a Danver, was the way she had patted herself on the back, and *he* was a Doane. A thick-headed lot, the Doanes!—to hear her tell it. Say, she was good. Hip-hip-hurray for old Ivory Dome, I thought, glad at the moment, though fooled, too, that old henpecked was coming out ahead.

Of course, to a point of detail, a number of things needed explaining—for instance the old man's trick of slamming the death-chamber door every night at ten o'clock. As for the "queer smell," he probably carried a bottle of it in his pocket. How simple everything was now! Yet we had let the "mystery" bewilder us! Fine detectives, we were.

"Pa! Pa!" Above me the woman's shrill voice rang through the house. Boy, was she ever yipping it off! "Pa! Where are you? *Pa!*"

Quick as scat, the light went out in the kitchen. Then I heard the old man coming toward me in the dark, sort of muttering angrily to himself. He was breathing hard, too. Like a cornered animal. I got to one side, flat against the wall. And hurrying up the stairs, the older one passed me without touching me. But it was a close shave, I want to tell you. Phew! Was I ever sweating.

Here a key turned in the kitchen lock. It was Poppy. The spy had gotten away from him, he told me, starting to strip off his wet clothes. Then, stopping, he looked at me and grinned. I don't know—when he grins at me that way, as though I mean so very much to him, like a ton of chewing gum, or something, it just seems to me as though I love him a million times. Oh, gee, he's a peachy kid. I hope I always have him for a pal.

"What happened to you and the flashlight?" he inquired. "Did you both go to sleep?"

I quickly ran through my story.

"I'm not surprised," came the thoughtful nod, when I wound up. "For, to tell the truth, I half suspicioned the old man of putting on, though I think he was dizzy enough right after the accident. Later on I noticed a sort of crafty look in his eyes, which set me to thinking. He'll bear watching, all right."

"Shall we tell Mrs. Doane?"

The other laughed.

"You must hate the henpecked old man, Jerry, to suggest a thing like that. For what Mrs. Samantha Ann *Danver* Doane would do to him, huh? Boy, oh boy! No, let's keep his secret. Then by watching him, and finding out *why* he's doing these things, we ought to quickly clear up the mystery."

I saw what Poppy meant. We knew what the old man was doing, but we weren't wise to his object. And to get wise was to be our job.

"Do you suppose," was the theory I then brought out, "that the old geezer is working with the spy, and that he came downstairs to-night to let the other man in the house?"

"That's a good guess. But it so happened that *I* had the door key. See? Hence disappointment for old Ivory Dome, and possibly, as you say, for the other guy, too."

"You didn't get a look at him?"

"No. I was within a few feet of him once, but he gave me the slip. I think he lit out for New Zion."

"Anyway," says I, "you wouldn't have known who he was if you had seen his face. For the people around here are all strangers to you."

"I could have described him to Mrs. Doane."

Having dried Poppy's clothes beside the kitchen fire, we went to bed, at one o'clock, and slept until breakfast time.

"Laws-a-me!" was the familiar exclamation that greeted us when we came downstairs. "It does beat all how some boys can sleep. I dare say you never heard me screeching my head off in the middle of the night."

THE GALLOPING SNAIL

"No," says Poppy truthfully, "*I* never heard you."

"Waking up suddenly, I missed Pa. He wasn't in bed where I put him. And where do you think I found him—*sleep*walking, mind you. Imagine! As though he wasn't dumb enough without trying *that*. Oh, dear! If he isn't enough to tax the patience of a saint. No wonder I have to watch him like a child. *Pa!*" then came sharply. "Quit gurgling in the wash basin."

"I wasn't gurglin'," whined the old man, as he fiddled at the sink, washing his face and hands. "I jest choked."

"Well, quit your choking then. Laws-a-me! For see what happened to your Cousin Peter when *he* choked. The poorest funeral *I* ever was at."

"I kain't help it if I choke," came grumpishly. "An' I kain't help it, nuther, if I *sleep*walk. No, I kain't."

*Sleep*walk! I suppose he was asleep when he blew out the kitchen light and beat it up the stairs! Yes, he was—like so much mud!

The old trickster!

CHAPTER VII

LAWYER CHEW

BEFORE doing our own breakfast stuff Poppy and I meandered to the barn and fed the big gander. All Mrs. Doane could give us in the way of gander grub was cornflakes in the package, but that seemed to fill the bill. And, to a point of nonsense, "fill the bill" is right! Boy, you should have seen that hightoned corn fodder evaporate when old peppy socked his molars into it! Part of the time the hungry fowl ate out of our hands. We let it do that, for, as I say, it was a swell pet.

"If only it could talk," says Poppy, "and tell us where it came from."

"A talking gander! You don't ask for much."

"A talking gander isn't so much more freaky than a spotted gander."

That was true, too. Certainly, I checked up on myself, in quick thought, *I* never had seen a spotted gander before, nor had I ever heard of one.

As though it were wise to what we were saying back and forth, and wanted to help us clear up the mystery that hung over it, the gander waddled to the

THE GALLOPING SNAIL

barn door, sort of eager-like, then came back again. "Urk! Urk! Urk!" it said over and over, deep down in its long upholstered windpipe.

I looked at Poppy and laughed.

"What does 'Urk!' mean?"

No sooner had I said it than the gander again left us and waddled to the door. Then, having looked outside as before, it came back to us with more "Urk! Urk! Urk!" stuff.

But we were dumb. Whatever its secret was it couldn't make us understand.

It was now up to us to sort of decide what we should do after breakfast. Of course, what we wanted to do, as I have said, was to stick around and solve the mystery. But we couldn't very well do that without an invitation from Mrs. Doane. For it wasn't our mystery.

"You said something about going to Pardyville to search for the granddaughter," I reminded in the course of our talk. "So how would it be for us to suggest that to the old lady? Then, whether we found the girl or not, we could come back here and report."

"No chance of us finding the girl in Pardyville, Jerry."

"You think she isn't there?"

"If she is, she's hiding. That's my idea now."

"Hiding?" says I, looking at him. "What do you mean?"

"Evidently something unexpected bobbed up to cause her to change her plans about coming here. And instead of being stranded in Pardyville, as we thought last night before we got hep to the old man, she probably stayed there of her own accord."

"And sent him back home with orders to keep his mouth shut, huh?"

"Something like that."

"Then," was the somewhat crazy theory that I now brought out, "it may have been from her that he got the spotted gander."

"I thought of that. But from every side it's a queer tangled mess. And least of all can I figure out *why* the girl should lug a gander to Pardyville with her."

"It may be a pet of hers."

"Possibly. But, if so, why didn't she keep it? Why did she send it here instead of coming herself? And what was her object in planning a secret trip here in the first place?"

"The old man knows," I waggled.

Poppy quickly picked that up.

"Old Ivory Dome! I'll tell the world he knows— the old trickster!"

"Maybe we can pump him."

"If you notice, Jerry, he does a lot of *listening* but blamed little talking."

I laughed, thinking to myself that the old man never had a chance to do much talking when his wife was around. Listening had gotten to be a sort of habit with him.

"It would be natural for us to think," Poppy then went on, "that he was working *with* the girl instead of against her. Yet he's fooling his wife—we know that. So I can't help but be suspicious of him, though I'd hate to think that he could be crooked enough to sell out his own wife's people."

"If he's working with the girl, then the spy must be on her side, too," I figured out, still of the opinion that the old man and the spy were linked together in their secret stuff.

"But why should the girl send a spy here?"

"She has old Ivory Dome working on the inside, and the other guy works on the outside."

Poppy began to pull his hair.

"*Good* night! Some tangle, huh?"

"Yes," says I, "and I want to stay here to see the finish. For I have a hunch that it's going to be exciting. So let us offer to go to Pardyville, as I say. We may not get wise to any real stuff over there. But even so we can come back to-night. And to-morrow morning another excuse may bob up to keep us here. If necessary we can *make* it bob up—clever little doo-dads that we are! See?"

Poppy grinned.

"Two souls with but a single thought," he recited, "two hearts that beat each other. Lead on, kid. I'm with you till Niagara Falls."

But I balked on doing the leading—that was his job, I said. So he set his planner to work.

"C. H. O. is closed," says he. "Therefore, as I see it, the only thing for us to do, in case Mrs. Doane falls for our scheme, is to hoof it through New Zion to Neponset Corners, where we'll strike C. H. P. It ought to be easy for us to catch a ride back to Pardyville, for with C. H. O. closed the other hard road will be crowded with cars."

I let out a yip.

"Why hoof it," I laughed, "when we have a perfectly good automobile to ride in?"

The other didn't need an encyclopedia to get that.

"What!" he squeaked. "Start out in Ivory Dome's old junk-pile? You're crazy."

"It'll be fun."

"But it's all smashed up."

"I have a hunch," I hung on, still grinning, "that we can make it run."

"Hot dog!" then came from Poppy, who knows real fun when he sees it, and away he scooted for the road.

THE GALLOPING SNAIL 75

So far as we could see, the old junk-pile hadn't been made any junkier by its tip-up. Putting the straight four back on its wabbly legs, we twisted the engine's tail and away it went—the engine, I mean, and not its tail—as sweet and pretty as seventeen rusty windmills trying to out-skip each other in a hundred-mile gale. It was a perfectly gorgeous racket. The envy that would shine in the other kids' green eyes, I thought, all swelled up with pride, when they saw us—and heard us!—on the road! Oh, baby! We had the world by the tail.

Handy around machinery, including wheelbarrows and bicycle pumps, Poppy soon got the hang of things. And I let old greasy nose fiddle this and twiddle that to his heart's content. He was tuning it up, he said—only he didn't say it, he yelled it.

Here old Ivory Dome percolated into the landscape.

"Wreck it fast," he screeched in Poppy's ear.

The tuner straightened.

"What?" he yelled back.

"Wreck it fast," the old man screeched again.

"What do you want me to do," came the greasy grin, "go at it with an axe?"

Well, I thought I'd die. For old Poppy is as funny as a yard of pickled pollywogs when he gets that crazy look on his face. Say, he's a scream.

"Why spoil a perfectly good axe?" I yipped, to help keep up the fun.

This "axe" talk, though, didn't jibe with the old man's thoughts.

"No, no," he screeched, sort of teetering around and waving his arms. "*Wreck* it fast. *Wreck* it fast."

Poppy gave up then.

"He doesn't want you to *wreck* it," I caught on. "He's yelling *break*fast."

So we saved the engine further immediate suffering by turning off the switch and went in to breakfast, where we managed heroically to get on the outside of four dozen fried eggs, more or less, and the husky end of a hill of bacon. There was other stuff, too —a swell breakfast, let me tell you. Talking and cooking were sort of twin talents with "Ma" Doane, as we now called her. Our tasters put us wise to that, all right.

During the bacon-and-egg vanishing contest we heard about "Ma's" dream, which sort of explained why her mind, usually so jammed full of worry, was now taking things easy. She believed in dreams, it seemed. And in this particular dream she had seen "Miss Ruth" in a pansy garden. Pansies, of course, were good luck. So everything was all right. More than that, the dreamer had been handed eight pansies.

"Which means," the dream was made clear to us, "that Miss Ruth is coming on the eighth of the month, which is to-day, instead of on the seventh."

Poppy got my eyes and grinned. The big monkey! He can be as crazy as the next fellow when he tries.

"I had a dream, too," he laughed. "I dreamt that I was picking hairy pumpkins, and when I woke up I had Jerry by the topknot."

"That's nothing," says I, not to be outdone. "In my dream I was a horse buyer. But I turned you down, kid, on account of your long ears. Hee-haw! Hee-haw!"

But our clever little act was wasted. For Ma wasn't listening to us at all. In her superior *Danver* etiquette, or whatever you call it, she was giving poor Pa "Hail Columbia" for guzzling coffee out of his saucer.

"I see," she then yanked the conversation around to us, "that you boys know how to run Pa's car."

"We made a special study of snails in school," I grinned.

"Laws-a-me!" came the quick laugh. "Isn't that the *craziest* name? Some boys painted it on the car as a joke—it wasn't us who did it. I wanted Pa to paint over it, for having the dignity of a *Danver* it embarrassed me to travel through the country in a four-wheeled billboard. But Pa's ambition is about as thin as his wits, so the name never was painted out."

Then, to our surprise, and before we could get around to speak on the subject for ourselves, the little old lady asked us outright if we would delay our hitch-hike for a day and drive the old car to town to meet the afternoon train. She was afraid to let Pa start out alone, she explained; nor did she want to go herself, having a lot of work to do. If we would go, she concluded, sort of begging us, it would be a big accommodation to her, and always and forever she'd remember the kindness and feel grateful to us.

Well, as you have a kind of hunch, Poppy and I didn't lose any time saying "yes." I guess not. So it was quickly arranged, with no objections from Pa, who sat taking things in with his usual intelligent look, that we were to start right after breakfast.

That sounds crazy, doesn't it?—starting out in the morning to meet an afternoon train, and only twenty miles to go! But you haven't followed us yet in the Galloping Snail! Bu-lieve me, what a fellow needed more than anything else in driving that mutilated old wreck, besides courage, was early starts.

Poppy and I, of course, weren't fooled in the thought that we'd find the granddaughter at the Pardyville depot. Dreams were the bunk to us, "pansy" dreams included. Either the granddaughter, having dropped into Pardyville on time, was now hiding there, to a secret purpose, or, to another view, had left there on the same day on a later train.

But here was our chance. You tell 'em, kid! On top of the fun of galloping around the landscape in the old four-wheeled boiler factory, without spending any jack of our own, we'd be back on the job, as Juvenile Jupiter Detectives, in time to clear up the mystery of the slamming door, and possibly a few other "mysteries" in which Pa undoubtedly had a clever little hand.

Breakfast over, Poppy got my ear as I staggered away from the table.

"That old geezer sure is a puzzle to me, Jerry. Either he's all-fired deep, or, to the contrary, gosh-awful dumb."

"What's on your mind now," says I, loosening my belt, "besides hair?"

"He knows that we're starting out on a wild-goose chase. But did he as much as bat an eyelash? No, sir! All the time we were talking about the trip he sat there as blank in the face as a petrified billiard ball. I thought maybe he'd kick about letting us use his car, when the trip, as he knows, is all for nothing. But nary a kick, or anything else."

"He wouldn't dare to kick," I grinned, "with Ma behind the scheme."

"What's that about 'Ma?'" came a light voice over our shoulder.

"Say, Mrs. Doane," Poppy then jumped into a question that he had for the little old lady, "did you find out anything about the gander?"

"Laws-a-me! I wish I *could* find out where Pa got that gander."

"Won't he tell you?"

"He doesn't remember. If I've asked him once I've asked him a dozen times. 'Pa,' says I, 'where *did* you get that gander?—now tell me.' But I might just as well talk to a hitching post."

"Did the man who died here have a pet gander?" was the way the leader further tried to dig into the mystery.

"What! *Corbin Danver?* No, indeed. As I recall, he hated geese the same as he hated sweet cucumber pickles and safety razors."

"And the granddaughter said nothing about a gander in her letter to you?"

"Miss Ruth? Laws-a-me, child, what *are* you thinking about to ask such foolish questions? Do you imagine that the gander *belongs* here?"

Poppy, of course, couldn't tell her that he had a hunch that the gander had been sent here for a secret purpose. For Pa would get it in the neck then. We knew a lot of things that we had to kind of tuck away under our caps.

"SO, YOU'RE GOING TO PUT ME OUT, ARE YOU?"
Poppy Ott and the Galloping Snail. *Page 85*

THE GALLOPING SNAIL

Here we caught the sound of hoofs and steel buggy wheels in the graveled drive. Was it the granddaughter? Poppy and I thought so. And a flash of disappointment came over us. What we wanted to do was to show our stuff as young detectives. And it would turn everything upsidedown for us, as you can see, if the granddaughter now stepped in to clear up the mystery. Yet we were curious to see her. That was natural. And in the general stampede for the front door, to welcome the newcomer, Ma Doane was not more than a foot or two ahead of us.

But it wasn't the granddaughter. It was a man—a big fat man. Boy, you should have seen how he filled the sagging seat of that spraddle-wheeled buggy. His stomach stuck up so high in front that he had to look around it, unable to see over it. Of course, I don't mean that *exactly*—but you get me, I guess. The point is that the man had started to grow *out* at the belt line when he had stopped growing up and down, and now instead of using an ordinary fifty-inch belt to hold up his pants he bought engine belting by the rod, more or less.

Nor was he fat just in one place. His neck was fat, what little there was of it. And his *face!* Oh, boy! He had fourteen chins and his jowls hung down like apples in an apron. The corners of his big mouth hung down, too, sort of grim-like. Bulldog stuff.

We couldn't see his eyes—they were buried in fat—but I had a hunch that they were a sort of grayish-green, like a hungry cat's.

The human elephant, or whatever you want to call it, had gotten out of the buggy, after a lot of twisting and grunting, and leaving the fagged-out, drooping-eared horse to sort of regale itself on the leaves of a lilac bush, was now waddling toward the house. Watching him, all I could think of was a dressed-up duck. No, I won't say that he reminded me of a goose, for I don't want to disgrace the Admiral by putting that hunk of human lard in the *goose* class. The Admiral was a true friend of ours, as you will learn, and this over-weight geezer, as you will learn, too, was nobody's friend except his own.

Yah, you guessed it. Lawyer Chew, the big guy in Neponset Corners—mayor, chief of police, church deacon, school director, banker, street commissioner and last, but not least, *money lender*—had arrived in the capacity of family lawyer to kick us out and lock up the house.

CHAPTER VIII

ALL ABOARD FOR PARDYVILLE

"Who is it?" says Poppy, as the waddler tried out his weight on the porch steps. "Mark Tidd, Sr.?"

"Search me," says I, wondering if the heavy watch chain that the over-fed visitor carried around on his vest front, like a young suspension bridge, was solid gold. If it was, he must be a millionaire, I thought.

"It's Lawyer Chew," the woman told us in a low voice.

"Quick!" laughed Poppy, remembering that this was the enemy. "Get the teakettle."

"A dose of hot water is what he deserves," came stiffly from the fearless little old lady, as she planted herself, sort of belligerent-like, in front of the door.

Having successfully dragged himself up the mountain, like a heaving donkey engine, old fatty stopped on the top step to swab his bald spot and adjust his scowl.

"Well, madam," he boomed at us out of his inflated stomach, "I'm here."

"So I see," says Mrs. Doane quietly.

"As I told you over the 'phone," proceeded old dough-face in his ponderous, important way, "you are outside of your rights in coming here to live. The late owner of this place instructed me to close it after his death and keep it closed until the complete settlement of the estate. So I have come to see that his wishes are obeyed."

Say, I wish you could have seen that little old lady swell up! As I watched her, grinning, all I could think of was a ruffled bantam getting ready to do its stuff. Boy, was my thought, if she ever socked her spurs into old goozleum the goo sure would run.

"I don't believe," came hotly, "that Corbin Danver ever told you to close this house against his relations. And I defy you to show me any *writing* to that effect."

"I know my business, madam."

"Then tend to it," was the slap that old fatty got in the face.

"Hot dog!" laughed Poppy in my ear, as tickled as a monkey with the cooties. "I guess she handed him a hot one that trip."

The visitor's big ears were on fire now.

"Mrs. Doane," he rumbled like an angry volcano, "I didn't come here to bandy words with you. Nor do I feel called upon to show you any *writing* to back up my position as preliminary administrator of this estate. His chosen legal adviser, I was given certain definite instructions by the late Corbin Danver, just before his death, and to the best of my professional ability I am now trying to carry out those instructions. As I tell you, you've got to pack up and get out of here. And the sooner you do it the better for *you*."

But Ma held the fort.

"*Oh!* . . do tell!" came sarcastically. "And suppose I *don't* pack up and get out of here—what then?"

"In that case, madam, I'll see that the law puts you out."

That was more than the high-spirited little old lady could stand.

"So, you're going to put me out, are you?" she cried, shaking her fists in the lawyer's pudgy face. "You and the *law!* I'd like to see you do it. Yes, you better back up, you big bag of wind. For two cents I'd twist your fat nose. Maybe you'd learn then to keep it where it belongs."

"Madam! . ." thundered the heaving volcano, as the lava slopped close to the brim.

"Don't 'madam' me. You're more lucky than you realize that I don't fly at you and scratch your eyes out. Such an insult! And now that you have had *your* say, Mr. Lawyer Chew, let *me* tell you something: The whole state militia can't drag me out of here if I choose to stay. Is that clear to you?

Not that I'm a person to oppose the law, but in this case I don't believe that you have any *right* to put me out of here. If Corbin Danver told me *once* he told me a hundred times that of all his relations there was no one whom he enjoyed having here more than me. I was welcome to come whenever I chose, he said. Nor did he say that his death was to make any difference. Yet *you* try to put me out! And this in spite of the fact that I was sent here, as I told you last night, by some one who has every right in the world to use the property as she sees fit."

At this mention of the granddaughter, the volcano sort of subsided. And there was a peculiar crafty look in the deepset eyes now.

"What is this that you tell me about Miss Ruth sending you here to open up the house for her? Is she intending to live here?"

With all of her free talk to us, Mrs. Doane was foxy about showing her hand to the enemy.

"I'll let her talk for herself when she gets here."

"Then she isn't here yet?" and instead of craftiness there was satisfaction in the gray-green eyes now.

"If she were," came sharply, "you'd have been ordered away from here before this. For while you may question *my* right to be here, I don't think, if you have any judgment at all, that you would question *her* right."

THE GALLOPING SNAIL 87

In the further heated talk between the angry man and woman, I got the feeling that it was a case of dog eat dog. They both hated each other. And probably, I concluded, it was to spite the woman more than anything else that the visitor was now threatening to come back in the afternoon with the sheriff.

"Nor will it avail you anything to resist. For I have the law on my side. And I'm going to use it. If necessary," came the final ugly threat, "we can take you by force and set you down outside of the stone wall. And that's where you'll stay until the granddaughter gets here."

Well, say, if he hadn't backed down the steps I actually believe that he would have lost what little hair he had. For take it from me that little old lady was *mad*. Drive her out of the house, would he? Set her down outside of the stone wall in spitework, huh? Gr-r-r-r!

But she went all to pieces when the angry lawyer was gone. She trembled like a leaf. And there was worry and every other kind of grief mixed up in her thin face. The poor old soul! She had tried to be brave but her age was against her. I felt sorry for her. And what I wanted to do to old fatty!

Poppy drew me aside. And as I got a squint at his face I saw right off that he was getting ready to do something. He's that kind of a kid. Let some one he likes get stepped on and he'll fight his head off for them. And now, as I saw, hating the lawyer the same as me, and wanting to fix him, he was getting ready to take up Mrs. Doane's battle.

"When did old dough-face say he was coming back with the sheriff?"

"This afternoon."

"Then we've either got to find the granddaughter this morning or think up some kind of a scheme."

"It's easy enough to talk about finding her," says I. "But how are we going to do it?"

Here old Ivory Dome percolated through the front door.

"Jerry, *he* knows where the girl is."

"Shall we choke it out of him?" I grinned.

"Bu-lieve me, I'll try it if necessary."

"Why. . . Ma," came in a worried voice from the newcomer. "You look all white. Be you sick?"

"Oh, Pa," came helplessly. "Lawyer Chew was here. And he's coming back with the sheriff to put us out."

"Um. . . What's he goin' to put us out for?"

"Spitework, more than anything. He says that we haven't any right to be here."

"But Miss Ruth has the keys. Her grandpa gave her the keys. And she sent us here."

"I know, Pa, but Miss Ruth isn't here yet. And

THE GALLOPING SNAIL 89

until she comes we're helpless. Oh, the humiliation if that man does put us out in the road! To think that such a thing could happen to a *Danver* at the hands of a man whose grandfather was a horse thief!"

Poppy and I were watching the old man to see what we could read in his face. For in this new trouble it didn't seem possible to us that he could hide all trace of his secret. Yet we saw nothing—only dumbness. I began to wonder then if he really knew as much about the granddaughter's hiding place and her other secrets as we imagined. Maybe, I admitted our error, we were all wrong in our belief.

Poppy had gone into the house. And now I heard him at the telephone. When he came out he was grinning. But when I asked him what the joke was he wouldn't tell me. I suspected, though, that he had made the first move against the enemy.

It was now time for us to start for Pardyville. So, with the old engine heaving and snorting, we loaded ourselves onto the cushioned back of the Galloping Snail and gallantly set forth on our journey, yelling to Ma Doane the very last thing to keep a stiff upper lip and cook a lot of beefsteak and gravy. For there'd be five of us for supper, we promised. Down in our hearts, though, we were saying "maybe." Yet it was all right, we thought, to say something like that to cheer her up. And it made us glad to know that we left her smiling.

CHAPTER IX

NO AUTOMOBILES ALLOWED

"JERRY," says Poppy, as we sort of hurtled down the sandy country road at the hair-raising speed of six miles an hour, or less, "that lawyer is a crook."

"He almost got his nose crooked," I grinned, remembering the fracas on the porch of the big stone house.

"He hates Ma Doane, of course—we could easily see that—but there's more than spitework back of his threat to get the sheriff."

"You think he's got a *reason* for wanting to kick the others out of the house?"

"Absolutely. He talked big about his *duty* to the dead man. But that was all bluff. 'Dollars' is a bigger thing in his mind than 'duty.' You wait and see if I haven't got the right line on him."

"The dope about the granddaughter's visit didn't seem to tickle him for two cents."

"I'll tell the world it didn't. And right there is where we pick up a clew, kid. He doesn't want her to come here and use the house. Furthermore, he doesn't want Ma Doane or anyone else living there. See? That's why he's getting the sheriff."

THE GALLOPING SNAIL 91

"He knows what's in the will—Ma said so."

"Sure thing. And if he's actually trying to keep the family of the dead man out of the house, as we think, it's a pretty safe bet that he's doing it to line his own pockets. For, as I say, he struck me as being an old money grabber. You know what I mean—the 'Shylock' kind. And I don't think he cares a whang whether he gets his money honestly or not. Men of his stamp usually show in their faces what they are. And the rogues' gallery never held a crookeder face than his."

"Maybe," says I, "he's back of the granddaughter's disappearance."

Poppy considered that for a moment or two, then slowly shook his head.

"I hardly think so, Jerry. For you must remember that he was dumb on her trip here until Ma spilt the beans over the telephone. And to that point, it may have been information that he was after this morning more than anything else."

"Information about the girl?"

"Sure thing."

"He didn't get much out of Ma."

"He knows that she's coming."

"Gee! I wish we could find her."

"I haven't much hopes that we will."

"But you said we would," I reminded.

"We'll try, of course. But we haven't much to work on—you can see that. If we do find her, or get the slightest trace of her, it'll be more luck than anything else."

"I always was lucky," I grinned. "One time I found a horseshoe in Main Street, and when I was picking it up Mr. Kaar's hearse came along behind me and wrecked my back porch."

But this clever little skit was wasted on old sobersides.

"Say, Jerry," came thoughtfully, "do you suppose the spy is a tool of the lawyer's?"

I looked at him, puzzled.

"But you said the spy and old Ivory Dome are in cahoots."

"Yes," he nodded, "I did say that—but it was just a rough guess."

"You're doing too much rough guessing," I told him. "You're getting me all mixed up. For if old Ivory Dome and the spy aren't working together, and the old man didn't sneak out of bed last night to let the other in, what *did* he go downstairs for? When I first saw him he was trying to open the kitchen door."

"That's so," says Poppy thoughtfully.

"What gives you the idea," I then inquired, "that the lawyer and the spy are mixed up together?"

"As I say, the lawyer doesn't want the granddaughter in the house. There's something in the will, I think, that favors him if he can keep her away. So, learning from Ma that the girl was coming, he may have sent some one out to the big house to stop her."

"Then the storm came up and the spy got his shirt tail wet, huh?"

"Yes, and a certain other guy whom you hang around with more or less got *his* shirt tail wet, too."

"You're sure," I pinned him down, "that the spy wasn't old fatty, himself?"

"Jerry! Don't you suppose I can tell a hippopotamus from a rat?"

"All right," I laughed. "We'll take it for granted that the spy was Lawyer Chew's hired man and not old hippo himself. And we'll further take it for granted that the spy saw you in the storm and got scared out. *But*—as the goat says, how about old Ivory Dome? Where does *he* come in? We know about some of his tricks; and we know that he's fooling his wife. I can't make myself believe, though, now that we've talked it over this way, that he's on Chew's side."

"Nor me," says Poppy quickly. "I'd sooner think that he was working *against* Chew on the granddaughter's side, though what his game is in playing ghost and slamming doors I can't imagine. It seems to me, too, that he ought to be able to trust his own wife. And to that point, you'd naturally think that the woman would be at the head of any secret plans to help the granddaughter, instead of *him*."

"Half the time," says I, "I think he's D-U-M-B, and nothing else but."

"Here, too. Yet we caught him in tricks. So it's all right for us to be suspicious of him. That dumb look of his may be just a sort of mask."

"Say, Poppy," I then laughed.

"Well?"

"I've got an idea about that gander."

"*You* with an idea! Be good to it, kid, for it's in a strange place."

"The old man was sent to the Pardyville depot to get the granddaughter. See? But *he* knew it was dangerous for the girl to come here. Old Chew was liable to cut her throat, or something. And so—"

"For the love of mud!" squeaked the listener. "What have you been reading?—a dime novel?"

"Anyway," says I, "old Chew was liable to do something to her. So Ivory Dome tells her to hide in Pardyville. See? And then she gives him her pet gander. And she says: 'You take the gander home with you. And as soon as it's safe for me to come tie a note to its tail—'"

THE GALLOPING SNAIL

"It's *tail!*" whooped Poppy.

"I mean its hind foot," I corrected. "She tells him that. See? And the scheme is for the gander to take to the air and carrier-pigeon the note to her."

Bang! Something under the hood sneezed its shirt off. And jumping for my life, I landed on my snoot in the middle of the sandy road.

"That's what you get for your crazy talk," the driver laughed at me, when I got up, rubbing my skinned nose.

"What was it?" says I, letting out my neck at the smoking car. "A bomb?"

"Carburetor trouble," says old monkey wrench, jabbing as unconcerned as you please at something or other with a screwdriver.

So far in this chapter I haven't said more than a mouthful or two about the old junk-pile that we were escorting around. Nor have I said anything to speak of about the road over which we were traveling, or the general lay of the country. As a matter of fact, in carrying on our gab, as I have written it down, we didn't "say" this and that—we yelled it. We had to in order to get our words into the other's ears. But I thought it might get kind of tiresome to you to have us yelling back and forth like a couple of loud speakers. So I wrote it down the other way—as though we were carrying on a very polite parlor conversation.

As for the road, if you can imagine a pair of wheel ruts across the most forsaken part of the Sahara Desert, that's the kind of stuff we had to travel over. Sand, sand and nothing but sand. The only place where it wasn't deep was where it was deeper. It's a wonder the old car navigated the road at all. And I didn't blame it now for wanting to lay down and rest —only I could have saved some skin on my nose if it hadn't used its sneezer on me. That was kind of unfair, I thought. For I hadn't picked on it.

As I have explained in an earlier chapter, this side road was a sort of forgotten connecting link between C. H. O., the highway that was closed, and C. H. P., the other east-and-west highway on the south side of the river. According to our map there was a burg up ahead of us by the name of New Zion, a community of "religious fanatics," according to Ma Doanes' line, and it was here that we were to cross the river. Two more miles of soft road beyond the river and then we would strike Neponset Corners, the town that Lawyer Chew owned—only it wasn't as big as he was—two hundred population, I think. Yah, you can see now how he came to be mayor and everything. All the voters owed him money, and

THE GALLOPING SNAIL

whether they wanted to vote for him or not they didn't dare do otherwise.

Well, to pick up my story, I bravely got back in my seat when Poppy hung up the screwdriver and crowbar. Then away we went again . . almost!

"What's the matter now?" says I, necking through the brass windshield frame to see where the engine had gone to.

"I killed it," confessed the chauffeur.

"Well," says I, ready to overlook the crime, "it deserved it. But you might have waited until we got home. For this is an awfully hot place to hold a funeral."

"Get out and wind 'er up, you bag of nonsense, and shut up."

"Use the self-starter."

"Say, what do you think this is?—a Rolls-Royce?"

"Yah, a Rolls-Rough."

"Well, show your stuff, varlet. And when you get through, fold up the crank and hang it on the radiator neck."

"Don't let the old tub run over me," I cautioned.

"Trust me, kid," bragged the driver.

"Have you got the brake set?"

"I've just been wondering, Jerry, if there *is* a brake. There ought to be one. But I haven't been able to find it."

"*Good* night!" I yipped. "Suppose we came to the top of a hill?"

"Oh, we can go down the hills, all right."

"Yah, I guess we can!—seventy miles an hour."

"Say," he threw out his chest, "don't you suppose I know how to handle this old bus?"

"My life isn't insured."

"Anyway," came the grin, "you aren't doing anything useful except rattle around in the seat. So when we go down the hills you can jump out and hold us back."

"The human brake, huh?"

"And when we're going up the hills," was the further job that was shoved at me, "you can get out and push."

"One thing in my favor," says I, "it isn't a hilly country."

Poppy and I have a lot of fun gabbing back and forth that way. It's crazy stuff, I know. But we get a kick out of it.

At ten o'clock we came within sight of a flock of dingy-looking houses. According to our map this was New Zion. The road that we were on seemed to be the town's main street.

A big weather-beaten sign jumped up in front of us. And reading it, we were made to understand why there were no other automobiles on the road except us. We understood, too, why Lawyer Chew had driven over from his own town in a horse and buggy.

I made a copy of the crazy sign. Here it is:

NO AUTOMOBILES ALLOWED

Our streets are privately owned, so we have the legal right to prohibit the use of automobiles within our corporation limits. Nor do we permit dancing, the use of any intoxicating drinks, card playing, the smoking or chewing of tobacco, or the playing of any musical instrument except the harp. Our laws and ordinances will be strictly enforced.

Noah
Jonah
Adam } Committee on Civil Affairs
Moses
Goliath

CHAPTER X

OUR MEETING WITH GOLIATH

THERE wasn't so much sand here. More black dirt. We could see stuff growing in a field. Still, it wasn't the best kind of soil—not for Illinois. And I had a hunch that Jonah and his gang had bought the land for a song. That is why they had settled here.

And what kind of people were they, I wondered, curious over the outfit, of which there seemed to be about thirty or forty families, all living in squatty, unpainted houses. Did the men and women alike have names out of the Bible? Had they dropped their own names to take up the Bible names? If so, was my conclusion, they must be a gang of religious nuts.

Now, don't get me wrong. Religion is all right— good religion, I mean. Take Dad and Mother— they both belong to the Tutter Methodist church, and when Sunday comes around we all dress up, as we should, and trot down the street to listen to the preacher—only I don't always stay to hear the preaching, though I'm always on hand for Sunday-school.

THE GALLOPING SNAIL 101

That kind of religion is all right. It keeps a fellow honest and square in his own neighborhood. He's a better citizen than the fellow who hasn't any religion. Take my dad again—you don't hear *him* cussing around like some of the ignorant dumb-bells who never see the inside of a church. I guess not.

But freak religion is a kind of side-show. It makes monkey-work out of stuff that God intended to be serious and sacred. Along comes some half-baked guy who thinks he's a prophet, and getting a bunch of simple-minded people together he starts a "heaven on earth," or some such bunk. And usually in the end he gets the people's money! I had a second cousin who got stung that way. A "prophet" picked him up, with the story that the world was coming to an end that year, so my soft-headed relation, after paying for his ascension robe, kept just enough money to last a year and the "prophet" got the rest. That sort of reads as though in my mind all "prophets" are crooks. As a matter of fact you don't find many of them doing business. And out of what few there are probably the majority really believe their own bunk. They're just on the wrong track, that's all. Kind of cuckoo, to use a plain word.

I read those names over again: *Noah!* I had heard of him, all right—he was the fellow who built the ark. *Jonah!* Every kid knows the story of Jonah and the whale. *Adam!* The fellow who ate the green-apple pie, of course. *Moses!* I wasn't quite sure about him. *Goliath!* Oh, yes—David and Goliath! David was the little wart with the sling-shot and Goliath was the giant. *Zing* went the sling-shot and *down* went old blunderbuss. Hip-hip-hurray for David!

"Well, Jerry," Poppy spoke up, and at the sound of his voice I sort of cut short my cheering to listen to him, "what are we going to do?"

"If we believe in signs," says I, "I guess we're licked."

"It's a wonder Ma Doane didn't put us wise to this," the other grumbled. "Blame the luck!"

"Sh-h-h-h!" says I. "Get out your popgun. For here comes old Goliath, himself."

Swinging toward us on high gear, with feet as big as canal boats, and dressed in faded blue overalls that were a mile too short for him, the giant, from whom I never once took my eyes, soon drew up beside our car. Say, that bird was *tall*, let me tell you. A regular walking Woolworth tower, and nothing else but. Nor was he skinny, like some unusually tall men. I guess not. His arms at the muscle part looked bigger around to me than my own body. What a brave little guy David must have been, I thought!

"Howdy, brothers," came the throaty greeting, and getting a closer look at the giant I saw now that there was nothing in his sun-browned face to be afraid of. "Come fur?"

"Ten miles, more or less," says Poppy, looking at the big one curiously.

"Pore road," the giant waggled, looking down the sandy trail. "Awful pore road. But then we don't need good roads 'round here, fur we never use 'em."

"Does that sign tell the truth?" Poppy pointed.

"Supposedly, brother; supposedly."

"What do you mean by 'supposedly?'"

"Wa-al," came shrewdly, "you're wantin' to git through town, I take it."

"Sure thing. We're headed for Neponset Corners."

"Exactly," and the voice was a drawl now. "Got some money, I s'pose."

"A little," says Poppy guarded-like, and he looked at me to see if I had the same suspicions of the stranger that he had.

"As much as five dollars?" came the continued drawl, as the man sort of bent over and studied our faces.

"I think so."

"Wa-al, then," came the quick decision, "it'll cost you an even five dollars."

"To go through town?"

"Exactly, brother," and the man rubbed his hands. "Exactly."

Poppy isn't the kind of a kid to lay down like a door mat and let other people walk all over him. I guess not. So you can imagine how sore he was over the holdup.

"And suppose we want to dance a jig in front of your skating rink," says he, sort of sarcastic-like. "Does that cost us another five dollars?"

"Um. . ." came in continued craftiness. "How much money you got, anyway?"

"None of your business."

But old Goliath found nothing in that to scowl over. Instead, he sort of grinned to himself, cat fashion, as though everything was nice and cozy in the back part of his mind.

"Um. . ." says he, digging puzzled-like at his hair, which hadn't seen a barber in sixteen months. "What day did you say this was?"

"Tuesday," says Poppy innocently.

"Do tell!" the shaggy eyebrows lifted. "Tuesday, you say. An' I sort of had an idear in my head it was *Monday*. Almost let two dollars git away from me that time. You see," came the further drawl, and the big boy kind of leaned heavily on us now, "fur small cars like this 'un, we charge five dollars on Monday, but on Tuesday it's seven dollars."

THE GALLOPING SNAIL 105

Poppy promptly turned on the gas.

"Good-by," says he, "we'll be back on the thirty-second of the month."

But the giant knew a good thing when he saw it.

"Jest a minute; jest a minute," says he, taking hold of a front wheel—and bu-lieve me, we *stopped!* "If it's cash in advance," he came down, "we'll call it five-fifty."

"Guess again," says Poppy, putting on more gas to turn around, though to no success.

"Five dollars even," dickered the wheel holder.

"Nothin' doin'."

"Four-fifty."

"Nope."

"Brother," then came the sad waggle, and the blue eyes shamed us, "you've got a penurious disposition."

"Yah," grinned Poppy, unable to stay sore at the queer old geezer, "whatever that is."

"An' furthermore, you've got a *selfish* disposition, my brother. Here I be, a pore, hard-working man—I've got to have money to live on, even if they hain't no chewin' terbaccy in it fur me, yet with money in your pocket you begrudge me this chance of earnin' an honest dollar. . . I don't s'pose," and there was a hungry, begging look in the giant's face now as he bent over us, "that you've got a plug of J. T. tucked away in some inside pocket, hey?"

The old hypocrite! For a moment or two I could only stare at him. Some fine religion *his* was!

"Three years ago," then came the sad story, as the giant, touched by the memory of his earlier life wiped real tears out of his big blue eyes, "I was a man of the world. Chewin' terbaccy, movin' pitchers an' a car of my own jest like this 'un. . . What is it, a Ford?"

"A Rolls-Royce," says Poppy proudly, spitting on his finger and massaging a fly speck on the windshield frame.

"Of course; of course. Never heerd tell of it though. Looks kinda shot."

"And it's shot worse than it looks," the grinning driver admitted.

"Wa-al," came the continuation of the story, "steeped in the sin an' iniquity of the world, an' with two wimmin wantin' me to pick 'em fur a wife, one an actress an' the other a church worker, I up an' made the foolishest move of my life, pickin' the wrong one, an' in consequence here I be in a religious penitentiary. . . Gotta cigarette?"

"We don't use 'em," says Poppy, wondering, I guess, what crazy junk was coming next.

"Any new wars goin' on?" the giant then inquired.

"Wars?"

"We never git no newspapers out here—they

THE GALLOPING SNAIL 107

hain't 'lowed—so I don't know what's goin' on more 'an a mile away. . . Douglas Fairbanks still livin'?"

The old fellow was dead in earnest. Can you imagine? No wonder that Poppy and I laughed our heads off. He had been dragged here against his wishes by his new religious wife, he said. And to please her he had let the leader of the gang give him a Bible name.

He was like a big kid in his talk. Some day, he told us, with a sort of wistful, far-away look in his big eyes, he was going to run away from his wife, of whom he seemed to be scared to death, and go back to the "sins of the world." Then he inquired about the latest prize-fight news, ending up by asking who was President. I wanted to tell him "George Washington," but Poppy told him the truth.

Well, it was fun talking with him, but we were wasting a lot of good time. Having sort of made friends with us, he confessed, as we further dickered with him, that the regular toll fee for going through town in an automobile was two dollars. If we hadn't been smart, you see, he would have stuck us for a five-spot, knocking down the other three dollars. As it was, we hated like the dickens to let go of our money, for to a boy two dollars is two dollars. But there was no way out of it. Paying him the money, we sort of rode in state through town, looking for Noah and the whale, but to our disappointment nobody came to rubber at us. There was a big community picnic down the river, the giant told us. That's where the people were.

Having crossed the river, we came to a steep hill. And how we ever got to the top of it I can't imagine. But we did. From then on the road was more or less hilly. It was a glad moment, let me tell you, when we got a whiff of the Neponset Corners slaughter-house. Hot dog, was our happy thought, as we cantered into town. The good old concrete now.

I easily picked out Lawyer Chew's house. For not only was it big like he was, but it had the owner's name chiseled on the stone horse block at the curb. As further proof, I saw a fat boy in the yard who was a dead ringer for old Chew himself.

Bang! went something under the car. But I didn't jump this time. For I had a hunch that it was a blow-out.

"Lawyer Chew will think that you're trying to shoot him," I grinned.

"Is that where he lives?" Poppy rubbered.

"Sure thing. Don't you see his understudy on the lawn?"

The fat kid meandered into the street to watch the tire repairs.

"Some junk," says he, turning up his nose—only

THE GALLOPING SNAIL

he couldn't turn it up very high, for it was too fat.

Now, if anybody else had said that we would have grinned. But not this young geezer. He was too much like his old man.

"Lookit!" I nudged the tire fixer. "We've got company."

"Is it human?" says Poppy, taking a sweaty squint.

"It's got arms and legs," says I. "Nice plump ones, too."

The kid's face got red.

"Don't get rosy," says he, showing us a cute little scowl, "or you'll get pinned on."

"Shall we kill it," says I to Poppy, "and put it out of its misery?"

"Huh!" snorted little roly-poly. "You better shut up, if you know what's good for you. And you better git that old junk-pile out of the street, too. For we don't want trash like that in front of our house."

Poppy promptly let out his neck.

"Where is it?" he rubbered.

"Where's what?"

"The *dog* house that you were just talking about."

"Bow-wow," says I, to help things along.

"I'm going to call my father," fatty then blew up, madder than a dozen wet hens.

"Don't bother," Poppy turned up his nose, "for we've already met him."

That put the kid wise, which proved that he wasn't such a hopeless dumb-bell after all.

"Now I know who youse guys are," says he, giving us a pair of evil eyes.

"Who told you, Lena?"

"Lena? Lena who?"

"Lean against 'er."

"You think you're smart," fatty danced. "But just wait! My father's going over to Garrison this afternoon to get the sheriff. And you'll hear from him before night—you and that other trashy pair out in the country. We'll show you who owns that house."

"*Egg*bert!" a woman called from the porch of the big house. "*EGG*bert!"

Fatty turned.

"Now we know what it is," I laughed. "It's an egg."

"Yah," says Poppy, "a *donkey* egg."

"Another crack like that," frothed fatty, "and I'll punch your face."

"*EGG*bert!" came the impatient call. "Do you hear me? Papa wants you to get under the buggy and tighten a nut. Come now, for he's hurrying to go over to Sandy Ridge on business."

"Yah," hooted Poppy, "go roll under the family carryall, *EGG*bert, and tighten some of the nuts in your head."

"Is there a county sheriff in Sandy Ridge?" I inquired of Poppy, when the kid had gone.

Reading my thoughts, the other laughed.

"Old Chew isn't heading for Sandy Ridge to get the sheriff, Jerry. He's going over there—so he thinks!—to draw up a will for a deaf and dumb lady with cork legs who read about him in the Police Gazette and wants him to take her money and build a home for crippled nutmegs."

"*Good* night!" I stared at him. "Are you cuckoo?"

"Don't you catch on, Jerry?" he further laughed. "To keep old Chew from calling in the Garrison sheriff, I 'phoned here to the house, getting his wife, and now he's heading for Sandy Ridge on a wild-goose chase. He'll be gone all day looking for the rich lady with the cork legs, so Ma is safe until to-morrow at least."

Our tire fixed, we went another block to the concrete, only to learn, in sort of sickening disappointment, that the road to Pardyville was closed. A bridge had been washed out during the storm, and the automobiles going east and west were hitting it along C. H. O., which was open again. Our only way to get to Pardyville was to go back over the same road that we had come, and then east on C. H. O.

I now saw that Poppy was worried. And I knew why. Facing another long trip across the Sahara

Desert he was thinking that we never would be able to get to Pardyville and back that night. Not that we expected to meet the granddaughter at the depot, but it had been a sort of vague hope with us that we would get track of her in town, for Pardyville wasn't a big place. If we didn't find her, or she didn't soon show up of her own accord, it would be all-day with poor Ma. And that was no happy thought for us.

Young fatty yelled something at us when we passed his house on the way back. But our old buss made too much racket for us to hear him. Anyway, his smart gab didn't interest us.

We never expected to see him again. But we did! And toward the last under conditions that were pretty blamed exciting, let me tell you.

CHAPTER XI

THE RUNAWAY

I think it was around eleven o'clock when we pulled out of Neponset Corners on our way back to C. H. O. We had been three hours on the road, and if we were as long going back it would be two o'clock before we came to the big stone house where we had started from. To get to the highway from there would eat up another hour. And how long it then would take us to get to Pardyville, we could only guess at. However, we were going to do the best we could.

"If only we had known in starting out," groaned Poppy, "that C. H. O. was open. We could have been in Pardyville by now."

"Yes," says I, of a sort of financial turn of mind, "and we would have twenty dollars in our jeans instead of eighteen."

That stirred up the other one to more unhappy thoughts.

"Good night!" he yipped, yanking the steering wheel just in time to keep our Rolls-Royce from kicking over a tree. "Do you suppose we'll have to cough up another two bucks to get through that crazy town?"

"I don't see how we're going to escape it," says I, "unless our gallant little gas chewer grows a pair of wings."

"The blamed robbers! It's a skin-game, Jerry."

"Nothing else but."

"Still, I don't blame old Goliath so much. He's got to do what the others tell him, I suppose."

"He tried to skin us on his own hook," I reminded, a bit stiff in my feelings toward the tricky old geezer.

"He didn't get by with it, so why hold it against him?"

"You seem to like him," I grunted.

"I feel kind of sorry for him, if you want to know the truth of the matter. For he hates it there. He said so. And for that matter what man with any sense wouldn't hate to live in a place like that? I'd as soon be in jail myself."

"His wife must be a regular old rip-snorter," I laughed.

"She sure has him buffaloed, all right."

"Some women like to be bossy... I hope I don't get that kind."

"You!" laughed Poppy. "I didn't know that you were thinking of getting married, Jerry."

I made a sudden grab for my smeller.

"Phew!" I gurgled. "Whiff that old slaughter-house."

THE GALLOPING SNAIL 115

We learned afterwards that the cluster of rickety buildings set back from the road wasn't a slaughter-house outfit, as we had supposed, but a rendering works. Old dead cows and horses were brought here to be boiled and then ground up into chicken feed. To judge from the ravishing smell the dead animals were left to ripen in the hot sun for two or three months before they were stuffed into the jaws of the grinding machine.

When we were in the thickest of the lumpy smell, the old snail started to shimmey, as though, with some such feeling as we had, it was getting ready to heave up its mechanical insides. Then it gave a final stagger and dropped dead.

"For the love of mud!" I gurgled. "Throw in the clutch."

"I can't make it work."

"What!" I squeaked. "Are we stalled?"

The other took that as a slam at his driving, I guess.

"Oh, no!" came sarcastically. "I'm just dilly-dallying along so that we can enjoy the magnificent scenery. And see the beau-utiful wild flowers!" he gestured, like a nut. "Aren't they perfectly scrumptious? . . Climb out, Jerry, and see if a hunk of the engine is dragging in the sand."

I got out, all right—and in a hurry, too, let me tell you. But don't imagine that I stopped to check up on the engine. Not so you can notice it. What I did instead was to hoof it for the back-line trenches, away from the firing line, as fast as my number eights would carry me. Let the dead cows and horses fight it out among themselves, was my indifference. Their troubles weren't anything to me.

Nor did Poppy stick it out very long, with the hunks of future chicken feed sizzling past his nose like swarming bullets.

"The beau-utiful wild flowers," I mimicked, as he staggered out of the smoke of battle.

"Traitor!" says he, and he kind of meant it, too.

"What did you expect me to do?" I flung back at him. "Stand between you and the wind and fan you with a perfume bottle?"

This last mess proved beyond all doubt that our luck had deserted us. Whether we had seen them or not, thirteen black cats had skulked across our path that morning. Nor did it add any to the joy of the occasion to have the leader and I growling at each other. Anyway, to our credit, we aren't the growling kind. So pretty soon we were all right again. And seeing the funny side of our crazy adventure we almost laughed our heads off.

"Whistle," says I.

"What for?" says Poppy.

"Maybe it'll come to you," says I, pointing to

THE GALLOPING SNAIL

the car, suffering in the thickest of the gas attack.

"How would it be," grinned Poppy, "if we climbed the fence and moved the stink factory?"

"I've got it!" I yipped. "Let's turn off the electric fan," meaning the wind.

"And we used to think that Limburger cheese was delicious!"

"And sauerkraut," I gagged in company.

At noon the thick smell sort of quieted down. Either the wind had switched or the supply of ripe horses was running low. We could stand it now to go back to the car, where Poppy got to work. And did any music, even a calliope, ever sound as sweet to me as the first healthy snort that came out of that old engine when the tinkerer finally got the jigger cornered that was causing all the grief.

But within ten minutes we were hung up again. Nor could we get anything out of the old engine now except the weakest kind of a wheeze. We cranked and cranked. Boy, it was hot work. Our tempers were hot, too. Yes, and our stomachs were *empty*. Don't forget about that?

Poppy was thorough. He unscrewed everything that wasn't riveted down. At one time we had enough junk spread around in the sand to build six engines. And the funny part is that the more stuff we took away from it the healthier the old gas eater sneezed.

We worked till six o'clock. Then we gave up. It was no use, Poppy said. And if you could have seen how greasy and fagged-out that poor kid was you sure would have had a hunk of pity for him.

What should we do now—get a garage man from Neponset Corners, or go on afoot? I knew something about garage bills. One time I fiddled with Dad's car and it cost him seventeen dollars and fifty cents to find out that my new way of attaching the sparkplug wires wasn't a complete success. All we had with us was eighteen dollars. And what could any garage man do to this old junk-pile with eighteen dollars? Certainly, with the big end of our hitch-hike still ahead of us we would need every cent that we had. So we decided to hoof it for home. Yet the thought of that long sandy walk had us licked before we started in.

Weak as he was, Poppy still had a voice.

"Anyway," says he, as a final effort, "we'll give it ten more cranks apiece, and then if it won't start we'll kiss it good-by . . and hope that in the next world it suffers as much as it has made us suffer."

"I'll crank it first," says I, seeing how fagged-out he was.

Well, can you imagine our great joy when the old hunk of iron, at the first twiddle of the crank, grabbed

THE GALLOPING SNAIL 119

the bit in its teeth and started off as friskily as a two-year-old colt!

"There you are," says I, acting big. "Any time you want it started, kid, call on a *real* mechanic."

"Quick!" cried the driver. "Jump in before it stops," and joining him in a flying leap, away we went down the skyline at our usual break-neck speed.

But the jinx that was trying to chloroform us with bad luck hadn't used up all of its dope. *Bang!* went a hind tire. That meant another hour. It was growing dark now. Instead of getting a look at Pardyville that day, we'd be lucky if we saw the inside of the big stone house before midnight. A whole day wasted! And the two of us done up for nothing, as you might say. No wonder we were out of sorts.

It was eight-thirty when we crossed the river. New Zion was just ahead of us. But the whole town was in darkness.

"They go to bed early," I yelled at Poppy, as we hurtled along like a crippled turtle.

"Without any picture shows to go to, or anything to read, what else can they do?" the driver yelled back.

"Maybe," I yelled then, "we can get through town without them catching us."

Quick to act on that thought, Poppy stopped the engine and switched off the lights, of which only one was working up in front.

"If we use our wits, Jerry, we ought to be able to save that two dollars. For instance," came the plan, "as soon as old Goliath stops us, instead of forking out our two dollars, we'll hit him for something to eat. Two suppers will be four bits in his pocket, we'll tell him. All right. When we get ready to leave for home the old engine won't run. We accidentally dropped a gee-whacker. See? And you go back with him to try and find it. That gives me a chance to beat it. And once outside of town, I'll shut off the lights and wait for you."

"Lovely!" says I. "And suppose old blunderbuss grabs me and takes the two dollars out of my hide?"

"Shucks! As soon as he hears the engine running he'll start back on the gallop. Then you can easily follow him in the dark."

"And how about yourself?" says I. "You'll be out of luck if the old bus stalls before you get away."

"If I put up the two dollars, he can't any more than bawl me out."

"All right," I gave in. "If you're willing to take a chance, count me in, too."

I got out then to jiggle the crank. And what do you know if I didn't actually fall over old Goliath's big feet. He had been standing in the dark taking in every word we said! And right then, let me tell you, is one of the times in my young life when my heart, as the saying is, did a neat little loop-the-loop in the roof of my mouth. For see how big he was! *Good* night!

But the giant didn't grab me and start twisting me into fancy bowknots, as I had feared that he would. Instead, as I stumbled, he steadied me as gently as you please.

"Sh-h-h-h!" says he in a sort of drawling whisper, to keep me from yelling, I guess. "You boys got here jest in time to help me."

My voice was gone. I had swallowed it. But Poppy still had his.

"Help you?" says he. "What do you mean?"

"I'm runnin' away. I hain't a-goin' to live here no longer, like a prisoner, an' have a woman boss me 'round. No, I hain't! I jest set my foot down. An' now that you boys is here, I won't have to walk." He started to get into the car. "Shove over, Sonny, an' I'll show you tricks with the steerin' wheel that I picked up when you young sprouts was jest learnin' how to wear pants as wasn't hitched onto you with safety pins."

CHAPTER XII

DR. MADDEN COMES HOME

POPPY and I were doing a sort of double-decker stunt now. We had to in riding with old Goliath, for he took up two-thirds of the seat. But we didn't kick, however crampy it was for us. As a matter of fact, we were only too glad it wasn't any worse. Think what might have happened to us if old heavyweight had been tending to business, as official toll collector, instead of scheming to his own escape. Br-r-r-r!

I guess, if the truth were known, we acted kind of simple. You know how it is with a fellow when he gets caught with his fingers in the company jam jar. We didn't know what to say. And every minute we expected old blunderbuss to get his memory to working on our trickery, as he had overheard it, and start bawling us out.

But to our surprise he was as nice as pie. Either he had completely forgiven us, we decided, or in some dumb way had failed to catch on. So it wasn't hard for us to put away our uneasiness. More than that, in our happy-go-lucky way, we brought out a

THE GALLOPING SNAIL

pair of perfectly good grins. And to that point, I don't know how any kid with fun in him could have ridden beside that old geezer without grinning. Say, that was *some* ride. First a tree would jump at us out of the darkness, then the corner of a house, then a hunk of sidewalk. It was a lucky thing for all of us that the whole town was asleep. For otherwise we might have been jailed for intoxicated driving, or whatever you call it—like the time back home when Paddy Gorbett drove into the Presbyterian church and started bawling the minister out because the garage was full of pews.

To a rosy view of things, how handy old Goliath would be, we thought, if the Galloping Snail got another balky spell. Big as he was, he could push beautifully. If necessary, with so much muscle, he could *make* the old engine zip whether it wanted to or not. So it couldn't put anything over on us. We really were lucky in having him along, we concluded. And most wonderful of all, we had saved our two dollars, though not in the way we had schemed. To this point, however, as you will see, our joy soon lost its jiggles. Like the man with the nest of rotten eggs, we had counted our savings before they were hatched.

Having navigated into one end of Main Street and out the other, without upsetting anything any bigger than the car itself, the driver suddenly remembered that he had a duty to perform and stopped outside of town.

"Boys," says he in that deep drawl of his, "we want to be fair an' square. Fur in startin' out in any undertakin', this 'un unexcepted, a feller never gits very far who isn't fair an' square."

"Meaning which?" says Poppy suspiciously.

"We owe the town two dollars. An' it's our bounden duty to pay it. Then we kin leave here with a clear conscience."

"Forget about your conscience," says Poppy quickly, "and throw in the clutch."

"No, I kain't do that. In runnin' away from my wife, I'll have enough on my mind without wantin' my conscience to further prick me in the thought that, through me, these pore suckers, who don't git six square meals a year, was cheated out of eight good soup bones."

The upper deck nudged me.

"I know a good scheme, Mr. Goliath."

"Um. . . Hopple is my name—Samuel Cassibaum Hopple."

"Well, Mr. Hopple," came the foxy plan, "knowing the layout as you do, suppose you go back and ask Noah if we can't have a special evening rate—a dollar and ninety-eight cents, or something like that. As you're leaving with us, I think the gang in the ark

THE GALLOPING SNAIL

ought to sort of set up the treats. Don't you?"

But old Samuel Cassibaum Goliath Hopple was no dumb-bell. Not on Tuesday evening, anyway.

"Um. . ." came sharply, to let us know that he was setting his big foot down and wanted no further nonsense from us. "You jest come across with that two dollars an' quit tryin' to work me."

"But, listen—" Poppy hung on.

"They hain't nothin' to 'listen' to. We owe the money. An' bein' an honest an' upright man, I hain't a-goin' to have it on my conscience that I skipped out an' never collected it. It's my last duty."

But Poppy was as hard to corner as a lost collar button.

"You say *we* owe the town two dollars. All right. How much do you weigh?"

"*Me?*" came in surprise. "About three hundred pounds."

"Jerry and I together don't weigh that much," says Poppy. "So, according to weight, you pay a dollar and we pay fifty cents apiece."

But did old hefty fall for that clever little scheme? Not so you could notice it. Nor did he let us argue the matter further. Put up and shut up, were the orders we got, so, though we hated him now, we "put up," as he expressed it, and thus saved our hides.

Taking the key of the car with him so that we couldn't skin out, he was gone at least ten minutes. But if he woke up the gang in the ark to deliver the two dollars to them, there were no distant lights or sounds to prove it. Certainly, we didn't hear any elephants or camels doing their stuff. The big boy was wiping his eyes when he came back. Even when a fellow's wife had the rolling-pin habit, he told us sadly, blowing his nose, there was a certain amount of regret in leaving her.

Then on we went into the night, the old bus rattling and groaning as though each minute would be its last. But it held up, which showed that old Goliath was bringing us good luck, even though we had lost our two dollars. So it wasn't right for us to hate him. Anyway, as I told Poppy, though the collection of the two dollars had seemed unnecessary to us, the big one had done what he thought was right. And when a fellow does that you've got to give him credit for it.

It was our scheme now to take the old geezer home with us and put him up for the night. Ma Doane wouldn't care. And with a "spook" to catch and various other mysteries to solve, it wasn't a bad plan, as you can see, to have a big guy like that on our side. If we went to Pardyville in the morning, he could go with us. Or if he was ready at breakfast time to go back to his wife and let her lovingly use the rolling pin on him, that was all right, too. We weren't particularly interested in his plans.

Presently we met a horse and buggy in the sandy trail. I thought of Lawyer Chew right off. That was natural. But it wasn't old fatty. Pulling out to let the rig go by us, and stopping for safety, I had the queer feeling, as our skinny light struck the buggy, that a pair of gimlet eyes were boring holes through us. Who was this thin-faced, foreign-looking man, I wondered, uneasy in the meeting.

Goliath then told us that it was Dr. Madden of Neponset Corners.

"I used to see a lot of him before he went to Europe. Guess he jest got back. Some one told me he was expected home to-day."

I had forgotten that Ma Doane had spoken of this doctor. But Poppy hadn't. Bu-lieve me, that kid doesn't forget about anything.

"Isn't this the doctor," says he, "who took care of the old man in the big stone house before he died?"

"Um. . . Reckon you mean Mr. Corbin Danver. Yes, Dr. Madden had that case."

"Is he a friend of Lawyer Chew's?"

"Who? Madden? Possibly. I kain't say."

"Do you know Lawyer Chew very well?"

"Humph! I know him by hearsay an' sight. An' that's enough fur me."

"You don't think much of him?"

"No, nor of snakes, nuther."

"Do you like Dr. Madden?"

"Him? Wa-al, I might like him better if he wasn't so kind o' *queer*."

"Queer?" says Poppy.

"He's got queer eyes fur one thing."

"Eyes that look a hole through a fellow, huh?" I put in.

"Exactly. He gives you the feelin' when he's around you that he's constantly *lookin'* fur somethin'."

"And you never heard," pressed Poppy, "that he and Lawyer Chew were particularly chummy, or that they were mixed up in any kind of property deals together?"

"Nope."

"Dr. Madden went to Europe right after Mr. Danver's funeral, didn't he?"

"Ye-es, I think he did. That same week, as I recall."

"Did you ever hear *why* he went to Europe?"

"It was told 'round here that he had gone away fur a rest."

"Why? Was the case out here in the country a bad one?"

"The doctor an' old Mr. Danver were great friends. An' I guess it was an awful blow to the younger one when the old man died so suddenly."

"Oh! . ." says Poppy, and his hand tightened over mine. "Then Mr. Danver and the Doctor were great friends, huh?"

"So I heerd. I know the doctor came out this way an awful lot."

"And did he tell around himself that he was going to Europe to rest?"

"He didn't tell *me*. I jest heerd it."

"Lawyer Chew may have told it."

"Mebbe."

"Did you ever hear," Poppy further questioned, "that the doctor had any pets?"

"Pets? What do you mean?—dogs and cats?"

"Yes, or . . possibly a gander."

"A *gander!* I never heerd of *anybody* havin' a pet like that."

"Neither Dr. Madden nor Lawyer Chew?"

"No, sir, nor nobody else. Them things people don't make pets of."

What was Poppy's idea, I wondered, in asking all these questions. Did he imagine that there was something crooked in the millionaire's death, and that the lawyer and doctor, living in the same town, were mixed up in some evil scheme to get the dead man's property?

Those boring eyes! Somehow the memory of our meeting with the man in the buggy gave me the creeps. Could it be, I further asked myself, that the doctor had known that we were heading for the big house, many of whose secrets undoubtedly were open to him. And didn't he want us there? Yet the man's eyes were naturally queer, old Goliath had told us. They seemed always to be *looking* for something. Looking for what? Did the *something*, whatever it was, connect up with the millionaire's sudden death? And had the search for the mysterious *something* taken the dead man's medical friend to Europe?—and this, within a day or two after the funeral?

Poppy, too, had inquired about pets. Did he have the crazy idea that there was some secret connection between the returned doctor and the puzzling spotted gander? And, further, did my chum think that the gander, granddaughter and doctor were secretly mixed up together to a sort of common end?

Crickets! Maybe they did connect up, was my jumping thought. For certainly, as we knew, they all had come into the neighborhood at about the same time—taking it for granted that the granddaughter wasn't more than twenty miles away.

Another thing, as the family doctor, the man with the thin face and eagle eyes knew *why* the millionaire had died; or, to put it another way, he knew what had caused the rich man's sudden death. The question was, did Lawyer Chew know, too?

CHAPTER XIII

POPPY'S AMAZING THEORY

AFTER he once got the hang of things, old Goliath wasn't such a fearfully punk driver. I've seen worse. Shortly after meeting Dr. Madden we very nicely tried to rainbow over a tree. And turning into the graveled drive at the big stone house we put on another sort of dizzy loop-the-loop stunt—two wheels up and two wheels down. But what was that? Nothing to crab about.

Poppy looked at his watch when we got out of the car and stretched our legs.

"Ten-thirty," says he. And from the way he spoke I could tell right off that he was thinking about the death-chamber door. As I have written down, we had planned on being here to-night when the mysterious door did its stuff, to sort of check up on it and thus find out what made it slam. But Fate had worked against us.

Old Goliath let out his big neck at the lighted house.

"And this," says he curiously, "is the shebang where we're goin' to bunk fur the night, hey?"

"This," nodded Poppy, "is the shack."

We had told the old man, of course, how we happened to be staying here. But he didn't know about the mystery. For we had no business telling that. Whatever he found out, we decided, we'd let him get it straight from Ma Doane herself and not from us.

Having heard us drive in, the little old lady came running.

"Why! . ." she cried, looking the gang over for a familiar face. "Where's Miss Ruth?"

Having failed her, we sort of hung our heads as we told the story of our hard luck. Yet it wasn't our fault, we said. We had done our best. It was a case of having too many black cats to buck against.

"Pshaw!" says she, getting control of herself so quickly that it surprised us. "You needn't act so sheepish about it. If you want to know the truth, I'm used to disappointments. A body has to be in living with Pa. For he's the most disappointing person I've ever known. He's a disappointment in himself and a disappointment in almost everything he does—except eat. And even then I have to watch him like a hawk to see that he doesn't bite chunks out of the dishes. . . Did you see Lawyer Chew in Neponset Corners?"

"No," grinned Poppy, "but we saw his son Eggbert."

"I don't know him."

"Well, you haven't missed much."

"All the afternoon," the woman went on, "I have been in fear and trembling that the sheriff would come and put us out. But I have seen nothing of him, nor the lawyer either, for that matter."

Poppy laughed. But he didn't take the time just then to explain why the sheriff hadn't showed up.

"Any word from the granddaughter?" he inquired.

"Laws-a-me! Wasn't I expecting you to bring Miss Ruth home with you? So how could I hear from her until you got here?"

"I thought maybe she might have telephoned from Pardyville."

"She probably will," came the thought, "now that she's waiting there."

"If she does," says Poppy, "you can tell her that we'll be over to get her the first thing in the morning."

All he said that for, of course, was to sort of put the woman at her ease. For he had no idea that the girl would telephone.

"Did Dr. Madden say anything about the granddaughter when he was here this evening, Mrs. Doane?"

The woman stared.

"Dr. Madden? Laws-a-me, child, you do say some *silly* things. For how could the doctor call here when he's in Europe?"

The leader told her then that we had met the returned doctor on the road.

"I thought, of course, that he had been here to see you about something or other. But he may have been coming across from C. H. O."

We then introduced old Goliath Cassibaum Hopple, explaining briefly that he was a friend of ours who wanted to get a bed for the night. We didn't mention his family squabbles, for he had asked us not to—it pained him to talk about the unhappy matter, he said, with sad eyes, and it pained him even worse to have others talk about it. To that point, it was all right, we thought, to keep his secret. It didn't hurt Ma any. How her tongue would have waggled, though, could she have known the truth! Old Goliath would have squirmed, all right. And it was just as well that he got out of that.

The doors were open to any friend of ours, came the warm invitation. But when the housekeeper got a better look at the visitor, and saw how big he was, she began to worry for fear that there might not be a bed in the house half long enough for him.

"Don't you fret none 'bout me, ma'am," the giant told her quickly. "Fur I know how to make myself comfortable on the floor. In fact, that's where my wife makes me sleep the most of the time, anyway—me and the dawg."

The dumb-bell! You should have seen Ma stare at him. And he had been so very particular to caution us about mentioning his home affairs.

"His wife," Poppy put in quickly, to smooth things over, "has some queer notions." Then he used his toes on old Goliath's shins as a gentle little hint for the other to dry up.

Going in the house, we sure made a wreck of the grub that Ma had waiting for us. Boy, did potatoes and gravy ever taste so good! Um-yum! Nor did Poppy and I shovel in any more hash than old blunderbuss. *He* seemed hollow from cellar to garret. Either his wife had been ladling out too much religion to him and not enough soup, or there hadn't been enough soup to go around.

Supper over, we went out to the barn with our flashlight, which was working again by spells, to see how the gander was faring, and finding it asleep we circled through the grounds to settle our big supper.

Another queer fancy of the rich man who had built this place was the fine lawn that he had kept inside of the stone wall, though beyond the wall, as I have earlier described, was the contrast of a forsaken desert. Hundreds of loads of black dirt had been hauled here to make a bed for the grass, and in the owner's lifetime there had been big patches of

THE GALLOPING SNAIL

flowers and a swell layout of bushes. I guess you call it landscape gardening, or something like that. The grass now was long, with a lot of dead stuff in it, but even so it wasn't a bad lawn. Nor had the bushes gotten ragged in the year that the house had been closed.

"Jerry," says Poppy, as we mogged around, "did you hear what Ma said about the death-chamber door?"

"No," says I quickly. "What about it?"

"It didn't slam to-night at ten o'clock as usual."

"The 'ghost' is scared of us, huh?" I laughed.

"We weren't here."

"I know, but we had planned on being here. And probably the 'ghost' knew about it."

"Pa's in bed sick."

"Ah-ha! No wonder the door didn't slam."

"Ma says his head has been hurting him all day."

"Maybe he tried to use it."

"I feel sorry for that old geezer, Jerry. I honestly believe that he's in trouble."

"Trouble? What kind of trouble?"

"As we know, he's mixed up in this secret, whatever it is. And I think that his trouble to-day is worry. Before we go to bed to-night, suppose we tell him some of the things we know and offer to help him. That may bring him out of his shell.

We'll have to do it, of course, when Ma isn't around."

Ungrateful bums that we were, the idea never had percolated into our noddles to stay in the kitchen after eating and help Ma with the late supper dishes. And finding her deep in the dish pan on our return to the house, we felt kind of cheap. Thoughtlessness like that doesn't get a fellow anything. So, to sort of square ourselves, we grabbed a couple of wiping towels and got busy.

"Mrs. Doane," says Poppy, as he cleverly massaged the gravy bowl, "did the thought ever come to you that there might be something sort of questionable about Mr. Danver's sudden death?"

A plate fell from the woman's hands into the dish water.

"Oh, dear!" she cried, looking frightened. "Why do you bring up such a dreadful subject at a time like this? Yes, if you must know the truth, I *have* been worried over Mr. Danver's death. I have had strange suspicions. And these suspicions have troubled and unnerved me more than you can imagine. Outside of Pa, I'm pretty much alone in the world. And, as I have told you before, *he* isn't much company. It's a waste of time talking with him about anything out of the ordinary. So I never told him about *this*. In fact, until now, I never have fully opened my mind on the subject to anybody. But somehow

I have a great deal of trust in you boys. And it *is* a big comfort to me to have somebody to lean on."

"You can lean on us all you want to," says Poppy feelingly, as he blotted a saucer. "For we like it."

"Yes," says I, looking into the gray eyes, "and we like you, too. And if we can help you, we're going to do it. Eh, Poppy?"

"You tell 'em," waggled the other.

"I've already told you about the night I looked in the casket. I was suspicious then about my relative's death, for I hadn't been able to get much out of Dr. Madden except that the sick man had died very suddenly. *Why* had he died? Heart trouble, I was told briefly. *Heart* trouble! Every person who dies has *heart* trouble. The heart stops beating, for some reason or other, and that's the end. I wanted to know what had *made* my relative's heart stop. But could I pin Dr. Madden down? No, indeed! He can be as close-mouthed as Lawyer Chew when he wishes. In fact, they're a good pair when it comes to *secrecy*."

"Do you suppose they're working together, Mrs. Doane?"

"Who? Dr. Madden and Lawyer Chew? Laws-a-me, child! They don't even speak to each other."

That put Poppy on his toes.

"Hot dog!" he yipped, flourishing the dish towel. And then, seeing the woman's surprise, he went on: "It's my hunch, Mrs. Doane, that there's a sort of secret bond, or whatever you call it, between this doctor and the granddaughter. But it didn't fit into my theory for two cents to include old fatty. So you see how tickled I am over what you just told me."

"Years ago," explained the woman, "the two men had trouble. I don't know what over. But to my knowledge they haven't spoken to each other since."

The leader got all screwed up then to spring something big. I had seen it coming and was prepared for a surprise. For I knew old Poppy! When it comes to *brain* work, I think he's a wonder.

"Do you know what I think about Dr. Madden's trip to Europe, Mrs. Doane?"

"No," came eagerly, "tell me."

"Like you, I think that there *was* something queer about the old man's death. I don't mean, though," came hastily, "that either Dr. Madden or Lawyer Chew are guilty of a crime. No, indeed. Dr. Madden, I suppose, did all he could to fix up the sick man. And certainly, if he had suspected that his enemy was putting across anything criminal, he

would have had the lawyer arrested long before this.
No, that isn't it. Whatever crooked work Lawyer
Chew is up to, it isn't poisoning, or anything like
that. Yet there's a mystery here just as deep.
And it was to clear up this mystery, I think, that
Dr. Madden hurried away to Europe. Now he's
back. And I'd be willing to bet my hunks of pie
for the next six months against a mosquito's false
teeth that he's got things all set to spring a surprise.
And a regular old gee-whacker of a surprise, too.
You say the will is going to be read to-morrow night
at ten o'clock. All right. Dr. Madden will be
here, whether Lawyer Chew invites him or not,
and you and Pa and everybody else in the family are
going to get the surprise of your lives. That takes
in old fatty, too. *I* think, to further spread around
my ideas, whether they're bunk or what, that Dr.
Madden is the one who sent for the granddaughter.
Right now he knows where she is, and at the
proper moment she'll turn up—to undo old Chew,
probably."

"Laws-a-me!" cried the amazed woman, with a
bewildered face. "You'll be telling me next that
Dr. Madden is back of the door slamming here, and
all the other queer things."

Poppy got my eyes for a moment.

"We kind of have an idea who the 'ghost' is,"

he grinned. "But for certain reasons we'd rather not tell you just now."

He meant old Ivory Dome, of course.

"And is it your idea," I asked him, when we were alone, "that the old man has been putting on this 'ghost' stuff at the doctor's orders?"

"That's exactly what I do think, Jerry. The three of them—the two men and the girl—are secretly and peculiarly working together. And the whole scheme, I bet you, is to undermine old Chew."

"Well," I grinned, "if they do scoop a hole under old fatty, I hope they make it deep enough so that he'll have to do some tall digging himself to get back where it's daylight."

"Dr. Madden knows his stuff, Jerry."

"So do you," I grinned. And I meant it, too.

"What puzzles me more than anything else," the other then went on, "is the spotted gander. For the life of me I can't figure out how it fits into the tangle, or why it was sent here."

"Ask Dr. Madden," I laughed.

"I'm going to," was the quick reply.

"Yes, you are—not!"

"We'll forget about Pardyville, Jerry, for in going there our time would just be wasted. Instead, we'll go back to Neponset Corners to-morrow morning. And we'll let Dr. Madden treat us for an acute case of friendlius-curious-snoopius."

But instead of going to Dr. Madden to be "treated," as Poppy had planned, it was the doctor who came to the big house, as you will learn in the next few chapters.

CHAPTER XIV

BIT BY A GRAND VIZIER

MA DOANE sure was a worker. The supper dishes washed and put away in the cupboard, each dish in its proper place, she got out a little comb-like machine for making switches. A switch, as you probably know, if you have any old ladies in the family, is a tail of false hair. Some oldish women still use them. It's a part of their dressing-up scheme. Camouflage, Dad calls it.

Switch making, we learned, was a sort of side line with Ma. She earned about a hundred dollars a year that way. A customer wanting a switch would save her hair combings, and Ma would take this tangle of stuff and make it into a switch with the aid of her home made combing machine. In talking with her about the work, which interested us at first, she laughingly told us how she had made wigs for bald-headed men, too. She wanted us to know, I guess, as much as anything, that *all* wearers of false hair weren't women!

After watching her for a few minutes, with the feeling that she was mostly doing this work to

THE GALLOPING SNAIL 145

quiet her mind, or, rather, as a sort of accompaniment to her tangled thoughts, we went upstairs to talk with Pa. For that was our plan, you know. To our surprise, we found the old man smoking in bed, as chipper as you please. Old Goliath was there, too, with another pipe. And in their new friendship if you think the two old geezers weren't messing up the air with tobacco smoke you should have been there to cut off a sample for yourself.

"Yes, sir," drawled the runaway, "it's the nature of some wimmin to be that way. They just kain't help it, I reckon. Not so much temper, I take it, as temperament."

"Or *dis*temper, hey?" cackled the other smoker.

"Exactly. Take my Clarissa fur example. She just seemed to have a natural hankerin' fur throwin' things at me. I didn't mind cold 'taters so much, or even soggy dough, though it were blamed oncomfortable sometimes to git some of it squashed in my face, especially when I wasn't lookin' fur it. But what I hated worser 'an that, even, was stove lids an' flatirons. An' to make it all the more onfortunate fur me, Clarissa had a most powerfully perfect aim." A big hand parted the brown hair that hung almost to the giant's shoulders. "See that bump? Some of Clarissa's fine work. An' that, mind you, is the very spot she aimed for, too.

Every *push* with that old gal meant a *put*. So you see, Mr. Doane, everything considered, me not havin' eyes in the back of my head to pertect me there, to say nothin' of gittin' soaked when I was asleep in my chair, it weren't sech a terribly useless or onreasonable notion of mine to skin out."

"Ma never throwed stuff at me much," came the second henpecked tale, "but her jawin' apparatus is the confoundest waggingest an' most con*sistent* thing I ever heerd tell of in all my born days. Talk about perpet'al motion! One day when her throat got stopped up so she couldn't talk I swar to Peter I thought I'd lost my hearin'. I stand her gab jest so long an' then I send her away on a vacation, so I kin git a rest."

Poppy nudged me as we stood in the doorway.

"I guess old Pop isn't so dumb, huh?" says he in my ear.

We had surprised the old man, all right. And listening, I was further puzzled over him. Was it a sort of lifelong game of his, I wondered, to play dumb in his wife's eyes? It would seem so, from what we knew of him and from what we just had overheard. To hear his wife tell it, he had about as much brains as a hitching post. But in the right kind of company, as now, and with his wife out of his sight, he seemed perfectly able to spread around plenty of fairly intelligent gab.

How shrewd was this trick of his, I then thought. By pretending dumbness he saved himself the job of saying "yes" and "no" all day long as punctuation marks to his wife's endless tongue wagging. Furthermore, he had no managing job as head of the house, for, of course, not being "all there" in his upper story, he couldn't be expected to do much work! Some men, you know, are lazy enough to jump at any kind of a scheme to save their backs.

Sort of summing up, I felt that I had a pretty good line on the tricky old man now. And I liked him the less for what I knew about him. Here he was taking it easy—and to that point faithful little old Ma undoubtedly had lugged his dinner and supper up to him on a tray!—while downstairs the innocent one was straining her eyes over a tangle of human hair to earn money to keep him in smoking tobacco.

Getting sight of us through the smoke screen, the two old gossips sort of rolled up their gab, as though they didn't want us to know too much about their family affairs, though why old Goliath should act this way all of a sudden was a puzzle to me, for certainly, on the way out, he hadn't been backward in spilling his grief to us.

Then Ma breezed into the room, jawing to beat the cars. *Such* a smoke! What would the curtains and bedclothes be like? Up went the window . .

and out went old Goliath. Not out of the window, you understand, but out of the room.

We grinned at him as he swung past us into the hall.

"I guess," he drawled, looking back with a comical twist to his face, like a spanked kid, "they wasn't no false bottom to that story of the old man's. She sure *kin* talk. They's no ifs or ands about that. She's what you call *pur*-ficient. An' between rollin' pins an' *this*, I think, fur a life's job of it, I'd prefer the rollin' pins. . . Wa-al, where do we bunk?"

"Jerry and I have the notion," says Poppy—only it was *his* notion and not mine—"that we'd like to sleep in the dead man's room. Mrs. Doane says we can. And she's going to bring quilts and things for you to sleep on the floor in front of the door, if that's agreeable with you."

Ma was bustling around in the smoke house, getting ready to go to bed, so Pa was out of our reach for the night at least. However, it wasn't important for us to talk with him right away, Poppy said. He had lost some of his sympathy for the old geezer, I guess. And I was glad of that. For it looked like a crazy stunt to me to show our hand to the tricky old man, as the other had suggested. He'd have us at a disadvantage then.

Eleven-thirty found us parked in our bedrooms for the night, Ma and Pa in their room halfway down the long hall, and the three of us in the "master's chamber," as the big room was called. A sweller bedroom I never hope to see. Say, it was more like a parlor than a bedroom. Boy, the carpet was so thick that it tickled our knees. And the bed alone must have cost a thousand dollars. It was *some* bed. Like a king's. On top of the headboard was a fancy doo-dad—a sort of red plush curtain, folded as slick and pretty as you please, with gold fringe. And there was more of the same plush stuff over the windows. The walls were laid out in big panels, and each panel was a separate picture worked into cloth. Tapestry—I guess that's the right word to use. The ceiling was a big picture of dancing ladies wrapped in strings of flowers—and bu-lieve me, all those ladies *did* have on was flowers! That was an awful side-show for a man to lay in bed and look at, I thought, blushing. The chairs had biscuit cushions and toothpick legs. Further, there was a table, a swell dresser that matched the bed, a grandfather's clock and a writing desk. Everything being new to us, it was an awful temptation to start snooping. For one thing, we thought, the desk might be crammed full of money! Of course, it wasn't money that we could take—I don't mean that—but it would be exciting to count it. Thousand-dollar bills, maybe. Millionaires *do* have thousand-dollar bills. Sure thing.

And having died very suddenly, the rich man might not have remembered, as a last act, to send his money back to the bank. But we didn't snoop, even though the thought came to us that among the packages of greenbacks in the desk we might find a private paper, or some such thing, that would clear up the crazy mystery. For Mrs. Doane hadn't told us that we could open the desk. Anyway, we couldn't have opened it if she had said so, for it was locked.

Poppy spent quite a bit of time examining the clock. For it was his idea that there might be a pair of hidden electric wires between the timepiece and the door. But he could find no wires. And we were dead sure, too, that there were no hidden springs in or around the door.

Helping old Goliath make up his floor bed, we tucked him in and then went to bed ourselves. The light was out now. And though I wasn't *scared*, still, as I lay there in the dark, I had a queer feeling. I put my nose against the sheets. They smelt all right. And just because they were *cold* didn't mean that they had been touched by dead hands. Sheets were naturally cold, I told myself. Yet somehow these sheets felt *different*. Sort of clammy-like.

I got closer to Poppy. If the sheets would only hurry up and get warm, was my thought. *What was that?* Oh! . . Goliath had kicked the wall in

THE GALLOPING SNAIL

his sleep. I tried to quit shivering. Those blamed co-old sheets.

"If you want to shimmey," purred Poppy, kept awake, "why don't you get out on the roof where you'll have more room?"

"This is a crazy notion," says I unhappily.

"What?"

"Sleeping here. What good'll it do us, anyway?"

"You seem to be getting a lot of exercise out of it."

"I've got a notion to get up and sleep with old Goliath."

"If he rolls over on top of you in the middle of the night you'll wish you'd stayed here."

"I'd rather be a pancake than an icicle."

"You don't mean to say you're cold!"

"Oh, no! I'm roasting. Get me a fan."

"But how can you be *cold* on a hot night like this?"

"Ask me why porcupines have whiskers."

"You and your porcupines!"

"Tell me why you want to sleep here," I pressed.

"For the same reason that a ten-year-old likes to monkey with the family clock. I'm curious to know if anything spooky *can* happen in this room."

"I'll never sleep a wink!"

"Kid, you aren't half as shivery as you try to let on."

"What if the spy breaks into the house?"

"Let him. We know who he's working for. And at our orders old Goliath will lay him cold."

"I feel better," I told him, after a few minutes.

"That's the stuff," he encouraged, like the good pal that he was.

"Shall we go to sleep?"

"Sure thing. For if we don't we'll be half dead to-morrow."

The sheets were nice and warm now. And how different I felt! That's the way it is with a fellow—he gets shivery one minute and then in another minute he's all right again. I rather liked it now. I felt like a king. What was that story in the *Arabian Nights?* Oh, yes! A boy wanted to be king, and one night the real king, in going around secretly, heard the boy wishing. And for a joke the boy was carried in his sleep to the palace where he was put in the king's bed. Waking up the next morning, he was king, all right, just as he had wanted to be! He was king all that day. Then in the dark they carried him home again.

That was me. *I* was king, too. And in the morning the black eunuchs, or whatever you call 'em, would come in, bowing and scraping. The Grand Vizier would come in, too, to find out which of my six hundred suits I wanted to wear that morning, and how many prisoners' heads I wanted cut off before

THE GALLOPING SNAIL 153

breakfast. Maybe I would be asleep when the Grand Vizier came. He wouldn't dare to wake me up, me being king. That is, he wouldn't dare to shake the tar out of me as Mother does when she gets out of patience with me on school mornings. Still, he might ever so gently touch my royal fingers as they lay on the solid gold coverlet. And that's exactly what he *did* do! He reached down and touched my fingers—only it wasn't my fingers it was my bare *toes*. More than that, he *pinched*. *Good* night! Didn't the dumb-bell know any better than to pinch the king's toes? I'd fix him for this. I'd have his head cut off. And *now* what was he doing? Why was he stooping over? Was he going to *bite* my toe? Well, of all things! I could see his white teeth . . and then, as he took hold, I could *feel* his teeth.

I woke up to find Poppy shaking me.

"For the love of mud, kid! Why don't you kick the house down."

"The Grand Vizier bit my toe," I yipped.

"The Grand Vizier! You've been dreaming."

"But my toe hurts. Something *did* bite it."

"Urk! Urk!" says a familiar throaty voice beside the bed. "Urk! Urk!"

The spotted gander! It was in the room. Some one had mysteriously brought it into the house while we were asleep. And wanting to wake us up, or so it seemed, it had pecked at the first hunk of flesh that it had seen hanging out of the bed, which happened to be one of my bare feet.

Poppy got up then and lit the lamp.

"You better get up, too," says he in a queer voice. "For there's no telling what's liable to happen next in *this* house."

CHAPTER XV

A SCREAM IN THE NIGHT

In putting the gander in our room, was it the "ghost's" scheme to sort of show us how helpless we were in the big spooky house? Not liking the way we were messing around in his secret affairs, and finding out things, as to-night, was he trying to scare us out?

Thoughts like these soon dried up our shivers. For we knew, all right, who the "ghost" was. Yet it puzzled us to understand how the old man could do so much "mystery" stuff without his wife catching on. She must be an awfully sound sleeper, we concluded.

As an excuse for getting old Goliath up, we told him that some one was in the house. But I don't think he understood half what we were saying to him. He was too sleepy. Then we went into the hall, where we met Ma on her way to the kitchen with an empty hot-water bottle. She probably didn't mind parading around in front of us boys in her nightgown, but I took it from her actions that it kind of embarrassed her to put on the show in front of old Goliath.

"Oh, dear!" she cried, glad, I guess, that we were there to listen to her further troubles. "I don't know but what one of you boys had better run downstairs and telephone for the doctor. For I'm having the *awfullest* time with poor Pa. It's that tobacco smoke. He's sick to his stomach."

Some more of the old man's trickery, was our natural thought.

"When was he taken sick?" inquired Poppy. "After he got up?"

"After he *got up?* Laws-a-me! I can't *get* him up. That's the trouble. I tell him he'll feel better if he goes outside for a spell. But, no, he won't listen to me."

"And hasn't he been out of bed at *all?*" pressed Poppy, in a queer voice.

"No. He just lays there and groans. Nor has he let up a single instant since I went to bed with him."

"Well, I'll be jiggered!" cried the tangled leader, looking at me.

At Ma's orders we lit the kitchen stove and warmed some water, which she poured into the rubber bottle. With this on his stomach, the sufferer gradually quieted down. Nor could we make ourselves believe, as we stood over him, that his sickness was put on. There was real misery in his voice. And his wrinkled

THE GALLOPING SNAIL 157

face was a sort of yellowish-white, like old piano keys. Such a look couldn't have been manufactured for the occasion. We knew that.

Poppy and I were sort of up a tree, as the saying is. Pa's stomach ache had upset the whole works for us. If the old man had been in his room all evening, as his wife said, then some one else had been secretly in the house. For certainly the gander couldn't of itself have opened and closed doors. No, it had been brought here. We couldn't doubt that for a single moment. And sort of putting Pa out of the tangle for the present, and suspecting the spy, we began to wonder, in growing uneasiness, if, after all, there hadn't been more deep *purpose* back of the crazy stunt than we had first imagined.

"What beats me," says the leader, as we earnestly talked the matter over, "is the easy way the spy slips in and out of the house. Locked doors are the same to him as open doors. And he seems to be wise to every little move we make. For instance, if his work is all on the outside, as we suspected last night, how could he have known that we were sleeping in the dead man's room?"

"It sure is ome tangle," I waggled.

"I'll tell the world. And *you*," he pointed at the gander, "are the biggest tangle of all."

"Urk! Urk!" came throatily.

"Wa-al, I swan!" old Goliath came out of a nap. "Where did that beast come from?"

"It belongs in the barn," says Poppy. "And if you can manage to keep awake for a few minutes longer, to help us take it back, we'll reward you with a beautiful celluloid stove poker."

I had a lot of new stuff in my head as I followed the others to the barn. As the leader had said, no part of the tangle was any queerer than the gander itself. It had been brought to the big house for a secret purpose, and furthermore it had been carried to our room for a purpose. But was this really an act of the enemy, as we had suspected? To take the view that the unusual gander was a sort of mouthpiece of the crazy mystery, wasn't it possible that some one, more completely hidden to our eyes than the spy, and more helpless than we suspected, was trying, in a sort of blind, stumbling way, to lead us into a solution of the mystery through the almost human-acting bird itself? And if we kept a close eye on the gander, in the barn, wouldn't we be likely to soon find out who the hidden one was?

This thought was new to both of us. And Poppy jumped at it when I sprung it on him. Here was our scheme now: We'd lay low in the barn, close to the gander, and then, at the least suspicious sound from the spotted fowl, we'd flash our light. In that

THE GALLOPING SNAIL

way neither friend nor enemy could come into the barn to get the gander for further secret stuff without us seeing him and thus learning who he was. More than that, we had a clever little trapping scheme, as you will learn.

There was a barrel here, and a clothesline. And how easy it would be, we planned, for one of us to hide in the barrel and do a trick with the rope through the bunghole. We worked out all of the details. Then the leader and I drew cuts to see who would have the bunghole job, for the barrel was seven sizes too small for old Goliath. Anyway, we couldn't have trusted him alone. He was too much of a sleepyhead.

I got the short straw. That made me "it." But I didn't get *into* the barrel. To sort of make it safer for me, I scrooched and let Poppy put the barrel over me, which gave me a neat roof. Then he tied the rope across the doorway and threaded the loose end into the bunghole.

"Now, don't forget, Jerry. You're to let the rope lay flat. I'll be in the haymow with the flashlight. And if I hear any queer sounds down here, on goes the light. See? I'll yell if I see anybody beating it for the door. Then you yank on the rope for dear life."

"And mister geezer gets tripped up, huh?"

"That's the dope."

"But suppose he's a friend, as I say."

"Well, we aren't going to kill him. And I have a hunch that if we don't stop him this way he'll skin out as quickly as an enemy. For he's trying to keep in the dark. So do your stuff with the rope. And old Goliath and I will be on top of him before he quits spinning."

The giant grumbled sleepily as he followed the leader up the ladder into the haymow. Such monkey-work, he said, just to keep a gander from being stolen. If it was such a *precious* gander, why didn't we take it to bed with us? What was the sense of losing all this sleep for nothing?

But pretty soon the grumbling voice died away. And how very quiet the barn was now! Like a tomb. Yet there was plenty of racket where I was, for the barrel acted like a sounding board for my galloping heart. THUMP! THUMP! THUMP! That's the way it sounded in my ears. Not that I was scared, though. I just didn't like being alone.

Squatting under a barrel isn't the most comfortable job in the world, let me tell you. I soon found that out. My bones began to ache. Nor did squirming around help very much. I thought of Poppy, stretched out on the haymow floor with his face in the ladder hole. How comfortable for him! Somehow I

THE GALLOPING SNAIL

always did manage to get the unluckiest jobs.

What was that? A floor board had creaked. As though some one had gently put his weight on it. *There!* A footfall. No doubt of it. More footfalls. Each as easy and as guarded-like as you please.

Then deep silence. The deadliest and awfullest silence I ever had known. What was the matter with Poppy? Why didn't he flash the light? Had he and old Goliath both gone to sleep? It would seem so.

The gander hadn't made a peep. So I knew it was still on its roost. Why didn't the man grab it, I thought. I wanted him to. Then maybe it would squawk loud enough to wake up the gallery. Poppy sure was a peach to go to sleep at a time like this. What I'd tell *him*.

Phew! Of all the funny smells. I got my nose closer to the bunghole. Some kind of a drug-store smell, I told myself.

The roof creaked over my head. And what do you know!—the man was sitting on top of my coop now. It was *him* I had smelt. Putting a finger through the bunghole, I found that I could touch his leg. But you can bet your Sunday shoes that I didn't touch him very hard. I guess not.

Ma had told us about "queer smells" in the house. On the dead man, too. Was this the same smell, I wondered. One thing, I knew it wasn't the dead man himself. For whoever was sitting on my barrel was a whole lot huskier in weight than a ghost. Besides, I had touched him. And you can't touch a ghost.

More footfalls! And louder ones this time. Some one else had come into the barn. Oh, if Poppy would only flash the light! What was the matter with that kid, anyway?

The man with the drug-store smell wasn't on the barrel now. He had slid down. And suddenly the barn was filled from top to bottom with the awfullest scream you can imagine. The scared-to-death kind of a scream. Boy, did my hair ever stand on end. Then I heard something else—a dull thump on the barn floor.

"Jerry!" yipped Poppy out of his bed in the moon. "Yank the rope—*quick!* The flashlight won't work."

Well, I yanked. I yanked good and plenty, let me tell you. But I guess I was too late. For nothing skidded into my rope. So, after a few seconds, I tipped the barrel over and got on my feet.

Poppy had seen me jiggle the crippled flashlight to make it work. And I could imagine that he was shaking it now to beat the cars. Pretty soon he got a connection. And did a light ever look so good to me as then. Oh, boy!

THE GALLOPING SNAIL 163

Scrambling down the ladder with the light in his hand, the leader looked to me to be all arms and legs. Farther up I could see old Goliath's slow feet. The light made a round puddle on the floor. It had found something and stopped. Something white and long.

"It's Mr. Doane," cried the leader, bending over the body. "Some one knocked him out."

Yes, sir, the long white thing on the barn floor was old Ivory Dome himself. He was in his nightshirt, exactly as I had seen him the night before in the kitchen. And his face was covered with blood. But he wasn't dead, as I first thought.

It was old Goliath who discovered that the gander was missing. But just then neither Poppy nor I cared a whang whether the crazy bird had skinned out of the barn of its own accord or had been stolen. What we were thinking of instead was the old man.

Carrying him into the house, we washed the blood from his grizzled hair, as it fringed his bald spot. The forehead high up had been bruised, as though from a club swat. Doctoring the bruise as best we knew how, and putting a bandage on it, we helped the vacant-eyed one back to bed, where his wife, as we could see her through the open door, was snoozing as peacefully as an over-fed kitten.

But she was out of bed the instant her eyes opened.

"Why! . . What's happened to Pa? Has he had another accident?"

"Hadn't you missed him, Mrs. Doane?"

"Laws-a-me! Do you think I would have been lying here if I had *known* that he wasn't in bed with me? Has he been sleepwalking again?"

Poppy didn't say anything. For that was better, he thought, than saying too much.

"I knew he'd fall and hurt himself," the woman ran on, to her own idea of things. "Oh, dear! Such a man! Must I strap him in bed hereafter, as they do with simpletons?"

Neither the leader nor I had asked the old man any questions about his accident. Nor had he mumbled more than a word or two all the time we were carrying him around and doctoring him up. For the most part he just stared at us, as though his whole brain had been stunned. Maybe, we thought, realizing that this was a much worse accident than the first one, he wouldn't have to pretend dumbness now. We hoped, though, that the morning would find him all right again. Then we'd question him, with Ma's help. And certainly we ought to get *something* out of him. For he wouldn't want to hang on to his secret if the rest of us were liable to get what he got.

As though the night hadn't been exciting enough for us, still another surprise jumped at us when we got

THE GALLOPING SNAIL 165

back to the big bedroom. The desk was open! And everything in it had been carried away.

A few rifled desks more or less meant nothing in the sleepy life of old Goliath, who already was snoozing in a heap on the floor. And after a few minutes, we, too, stretched out on the bed to get some rest. But we didn't figure on going to sleep. After all the excitement it didn't seem possible to us that we could. And to be ready in a jiffy, no matter what bobbed up, we kept our clothes on, even our shoes.

CHAPTER XVI

GETTING CLOSER TO THE SECRET

ARE you all tangled up in the mystery now? Having read this far, is the cart, in your jumbled mind, pulling the horse? Or, having carefully chewed up and digested Poppy's wild theory, together with the mess of stuff that led up to that theory, do you have similar fixed ideas about the millionaire's death, to start with, and all the other more or less hitched-together things, including the granddaughter's disappearance and the spotted gander?

What stumped Poppy and I right now was the sort of *contradictory* side of the crazy tangle. There was old Ivory Dome. Having surprised him in the kitchen, very "ghostlike" indeed in his long white nightshirt, we had jumped to the natural conclusion that he was back of all the "spooky" stuff that was going on in the house. But now we knew differently. The old man wasn't the "ghost," as we had suspected. He had secrets, of course. And maybe he knew who the "ghost" was. But it was plain to be seen, from what had just happened in the barn, that the two men weren't pulling together in the same harness. For if they had been, one wouldn't have knocked the other cuckoo.

No, whatever peril there was coiled up, serpent-like, inside of the queer house, and on its doorsteps, the old man, instead of being safe in his secrets, had as much to dodge as either of us. And, as I have written down in the tail-end of the preceding chapter, it was our scheme to use this as a sort of crowbar to pry him out of his hole. We had a good excuse now to get after him, roughshod, if necessary, and *make* him tell what he knew. And remembering how he was tricking his wife with his pretended dumbness, largely to his own lazy comfort, we didn't care a whangdoodle whether, like Mrs. Goliath, she cleaned up on him with a rolling-pin or not. She couldn't give him anything that he didn't deserve.

Yet, until we had the true story, it was interesting to sort of speculate, detective-like, on his motives and hidden actions. There was his trip to Pardyville. Having been sent to town to get the expected granddaughter, he had come home, hours late, with a strange spotted gander, now the very center of the crazy tangle. Meeting the granddaughter, had she put him wise to the fact that there was a bigger hunk of peril in the queer house than either he or his wife had suspected? After his talk with her, did he know *why* the death-chamber door slammed every night at ten o'clock, and what made it slam? And was it due to a scheme of hers that he had lugged home the spotted gander? Had she given him the gander, in completing her plans to "disappear," or had she told him where to get it, and why he *should* get it—further, why he should do all these things and *keep his mouth shut*, both on her secrets, as she had handed them over to him, and on her hiding place?

It was Poppy's notion that Dr. Madden, in planning a sort of exposure, had sent for the girl, as her friend. So old Ivory Dome, in meeting the granddaughter at the depot, could very well have talked over certain plans with the returned doctor, too—might even have gotten the gander from the other man, in fact. If so, was it a sort of *royal* gander, or something like that? And having been brought to America by the doctor, was it considered a big feature in the hidden scheme that its owner was secretly working on?—a scheme, of course, in which old Ivory Dome, like the granddaughter, was playing an important part.

Good night! I'd be thinking next, was the way in which I checked up on my crazy thoughts, that the peculiar gander actually had something to do with the millionaire's sudden death!

Getting back to more sensible stuff, I followed old Ivory Dome in my mind, from the time he had arrived with the gander until his sort of fatal trip to the barn. I couldn't recall that he had made any fuss over the gander. And that sort of contradicted the theory that he had been told to bring it home, as important, and take care of it. If anything, he had sort of neglected it. Queer. One thing didn't jibe with the other at all. And least of all could I figure out *why* the gander had been turned over to the old man if either the granddaughter or the doctor wanted to be sure of it.

In further spotting the dumb-acting one in the tangle, we had it on him that he had done two distinctly mysterious things since his return from Pardyville, not including the little side trip that had kept him on the road until ten-thirty: That same night he had slipped out of bed to unlock the kitchen door, craftily letting on, when caught by his awakened wife, that he was "sleepwalking." And to-night he had repeated the stunt, getting as far away from his bed as the barn. Was he doing this midnight shirt-tail stuff at the granddaughter's orders? If so, what was the big idea? Why did he have to wait until his wife was asleep to go to the barn? And what was there out back to draw him, in the first place? The gander probably. But *why* all the midnight secrecy? Further, had he been trying to get out of the house, to go to the barn, where the gander was, when I had seen him in the kitchen? Very likely.

But the locked door had stopped him. And the reason why he had growled under his breath, when he heard his wife, was because he knew that all chances of doing any secret stuff that night were gone.

But to-night he had pulled the trick to his satisfaction. His wife sound asleep, he had crept out of the bedroom, very well pleased, no doubt, to find that the kitchen door was already unlocked for him. And that he couldn't have suspected that anybody else was in the barn ahead of him, least of all a hidden enemy, was shown by his open actions. The first man had sort of *crept* into the barn. On tiptoes. But old Ivory Dome had stepped in as bold as brass. Then had come the scream . . and to me this was the most dizzy part of all. For it wasn't the old man who had screamed. No. *He* had been struck on the head, as we know, but it was the other man who had done the screaming. Yet, if you can figure out any sensible reason *why* the man with the drugstore smell should scream, womanlike, as though he was scared out of his wits, you're a heap smarter than me.

And now the gander was gone. The man had it, of course. But if he had come to the barn purposely to get it, why had he hung around so long in the dark? Could it be that he had hid there, as an enemy, to get a secret crack at the other man? It would seem so. But how could he have known that at midnight old Ivory Dome would put on the usual shirt-tail parade stuff? And, to repeat, having done the intended biffing act, why had *he* screamed, and not the biffed man, himself?

You can see how puzzling it was for us. Whatever theory we dug out of our minds, there was something to *contradict* it. But of this we were dead sure: Someone, as mysterious in his hidden movements as any real ghost could have been, was secretly working in and around the big house. Yet even there we met with contradiction. For if the hidden man really had wanted the gander, as his trip to the barn suggested, why hadn't he kept it when he had it earlier in the evening, instead of putting it in our room? And knowing that we were in the barn, why had he risked capture by tagging us there? Again, if he was so dead eager to put a dent in old Ivory Dome's thick skull, why hadn't he taken the easier and surer course of biffing the marked man while he was asleep?

It was Poppy's further theory that the gander had been put in our room to get us away, so that the desk could be secretly cleaned out. And there again was *more* contradiction. For if the hidden man had wanted to work at the desk, why had he followed us to the barn? Still, was our conclusion, it probably hadn't taken him many minutes to pry open the desk—only we learned, on getting up, that a key had been used to open the desk and not a jimmy.

And what had been taken out of the desk? Money? We had talked excitedly of thousand-dollar bills. But we really didn't know that there was any money in the locked desk. And now that I gave the matter more thought, realizing how the house had been closed and thus left at the mercy of tramps, I began to lose faith in the "money" idea. No, instead of money, it was secret papers that the man was after. And so as not to overlook the particular paper that he wanted, he had taken everything. But how queer, was my thought here, that he had waited until the *last night* before the reading of the will to clean out the desk! To believe Mrs. Doane's story of slamming doors and mysterious footfalls, the "ghost" of the big house had been secretly at work for more than a week. Why then had he waited until to-night to rob the dead man's desk? A spy of Lawyer Chew's, if that theory still held, had he been given orders at the last minute to grab everything in sight?

If only we could have known all this truck ahead of time! Then, on spotting the spy in the storm, we could have made sure about his capture, even to going after him in a desperate way. And to that point, with the house open to him, why had he stayed

THE GALLOPING SNAIL 173

outside in the wind and rain? That, too, was puzzling.

There now! If *that* doesn't completely tangle you up, I guess you had better go into the detective business yourself. But clever as you are, don't be too blamed sure of yourself! For a whale of a surprise may jump out at you in the tail-end.

As I say, Poppy and I had no intention of going to sleep. But when a boy is completely fagged out, he drops off in spite of himself. And that's the way it was with us, though we did a lot of talking back and forth, as I have just written down in my own way, before sleep got the best of us. Nor did we wake up to find our heads in one corner of the big room and our arms and legs in another, or Goliath's, either. In her own room further down the hall, Ma was bustling around, talking a blue streak, as usual, so we knew that everything was all right over there— only we were to learn at breakfast time that the injured shirt-tail parader, on top of being lightheaded, had itchy spots all over his back.

But Ma wasn't as much upset over the old man's new itchiness, and the disturbing truck that had come ahead of it, as you might imagine. This was a big day for the little old lady. Soon now she would know, in the reading of the will, how the dead man's property was going to be dished out. And, bu-lieve me, she wasn't bashful about speaking up for herself!

"One time," she told us, as she twiddled the bacon and eggs in the frying pan, "Mr. Danver promised me the red-plush settee in the hall. For, as I hinted to him at Aunt Samantha's funeral, it was a perfect match for the parlor suit that the other relative left to me—only this one piece, I dare say, cost twice as much as all five of Aunt Samantha's pieces put together. So I hope he didn't forget about the settee when he was making out his will. If only I was *sure*, I'd have you boys crate it this morning. Still, I better wait. For I may get a lot more things than I figure on."

Having washed ourselves, Poppy and I skinned up the back stairs, while we were waiting for breakfast, to see what we could pump out of the old man.

"Good morning, Mr. Doane," says the leader, when we were beside the sick bed. "Feeling better to-day?"

The squirming invalid looked at us with eyes that didn't seem to see us.

"Heh?" he fumbled vacantly, moving over in bed so that he could scratch his itchy back on a corner of the headboard.

"How's your head?" says Poppy.

"Heh?" with more back scratching.

"Ah! . . Come out of it. We know you aren't as dumb as you let on."

THE GALLOPING SNAIL

"Heh?" as the itchy one tried the other corner of the headboard for a change.

"Tell him to put on a new record," I grinned.

"Did you know," Poppy then tried to catch the old man by surprise, "that Miss Ruth is downstairs?"

But the only answer that we got was a dumb and itchy "Heh?" So we gave it up. For you can't squeeze water out of a sponge when the sponge is petrified.

"Say, Mrs. Doane," says Poppy, during breakfast, "do you have a key to the desk in the room where we slept last night?"

"What! *Me* have a key to the desk where Corbin Danver kept his private papers? Laws-a-me, *no!* Why do you ask that?" Then, in sudden stiff suspicion: "Have you boys been snooping in that desk?"

"No," says Poppy truthfully. Then he asked further. "Who has the key?—Lawyer Chew?"

"Outside of what keys you see here in the doors, the rest, from all over the house, were sent to Miss Ruth by registered mail."

"Who mailed the keys to her?—Lawyer Chew?"

"No, Dr. Madden."

"Maybe he kept out one or two."

"I can't say that he didn't, but I don't believe it. For he was too loyal a friend of my dead relative's to fail, in the smallest way, to carry out the dying man's final wishes."

"Then you think Miss Ruth has the desk key?"

"She sent me a few keys, when she wrote and asked me to come here and open up the house for her. I imagine she has all the rest, the desk key included."

"Can you think of any reason," Poppy then sprung the question, "why she should send some one here, with the key, to rob the desk just before her grandfather's will was read?"

Staring, the woman started to say something, to better get the leader's meaning, I imagine. Then, on a call from above, she dropped her breakfast and flew up the stairs to the sick room, where the unlucky invalid, in trying to doctor his itchy back, had gotten the ammonia bottle by mistake. From the way he was yipping and dancing around, his back was the next thing to being on fire, I guess.

Dr. Madden was called at nine o'clock, for the sick man was in bad shape now, and when Poppy and I learned that the family doctor was already on his way to the big house, having left his own home before eight o'clock, we had the jumpy feeling that something big was getting ready to drop.

While we were waiting, eager-like, for the doctor to drive in, the leader and I went to the barn. The gander was gone, all right. There was no doubt about that. In looking around for possible clews, we discovered a small room, without windows, that seemed to be a sort of storage place for empty bottles, the most of which were of the same size and shape.

"Phew!" gagged Poppy, pulling a cork. "Smells like rotten eggs."

Getting a whiff, I quickly took down several bottles, smelling of them one after another, convinced now that we were getting closer to a solution of the mystery. For here was the same smell that had come to me through the bunghole!—and probably the same smell that Mrs. Doane had noticed in the house, and on the dead man!

Poppy was excited when I told him. Then, in further quick detective work, we made the most amazing discovery of all.

Shoved into a dark corner of the room was a corrugated-paper box filled with bottles that hadn't been opened. There appeared to be a dozen of the bottles, all packed carefully in excelsior. The liquid, we saw, taking a bottle into the light, was red, like blood. But what excited us, more than the discovery of the filled bottles, was the name on the box cover. Here it is:

> Dr. A. J. Neddam,
> Sandy Ridge,
> Illinois.

Do you catch on! NEDDAM was MADDEN turned around. And more, there was a shipping date marked on the box which showed that the package had been taken out of the express office and brought here in June . . not the June *before* the millionaire had died so suddenly, but the last June on the calendar.

How could Dr. Madden, in ordering the medicine under a hidden name, and to probably secret purposes, have brought it here when he was in Europe? The answer was, of course, that he hadn't been in Europe at all! And with his own Neponset Corners home closed, it was as plain as the nose on our face—or should I say noses?—that he had been secretly living *here*.

So *he* was the "ghost!"

CHAPTER XVII

IN QUARANTINE

Boy, were we ever excited! And did we ever feel like yipping out a string of "Hip-hip-hurray-for-our-side" stuff! For now, as you can see, we had the cat by the tail. And soon it would be eating out of our hands—meaning the whole cat, of course, and not just its tail.

Yes, sir, clever little sleuthing doo-dads that we were, we had the goods on old "Mr. Ghost." And to think that the mysterious "spook" was the one man in the tangle whom we hadn't even suspected! However, that wasn't anything against our work. For not the slightest thing had bobbed up to hint to us that the family doctor wasn't in Europe, as everybody in the neighborhood believed.

Here is the dope as we had it spread out in our minds now: To solve the secret that clouded the millionaire's death, and probably to please the dying man, the loyal family doctor had hidden himself for a year in the closed house. There was deep mystery in his actions, of course, but he would clear that up. Sharing certain unusual secrets with the dead man, and an enemy of the scheming lawyer's, he had kept in touch with the granddaughter, and now was working with her, to fix it so the lawyer couldn't do any cheating stuff.

It was puzzling, of course, to understand why the hidden man, in his friendly work, had slammed doors to scare the two old people away, when the granddaughter, whom he was helping, had sent them here. But that wasn't anything. Maybe a queer broken brain, before it turned cold, had given the hider his orders. Certainly, the "queer smell" was easily explained. Every time the man went through the hall he had left a trail behind him, just as I had noticed the smell when he was roosting on my barrel coop.

But more puzzling than anything else—*contradictory*, even—was old Ivory Dome's swat on the head. You can see what I mean. If the two men and the girl were secretly working together, why had one of the men soaked the other as though he wanted to lay him cold? And that stormy night, why had the hidden one left the house, of which he seemed to have secret ways of getting in and out? Further, where did the crazy gander come in under the new order of things and who really had it?

Bu-lieve me, we were on our toes now for the strange doctor to show up. Not that we expected

THE GALLOPING SNAIL 181

to corner him with our dope. But we had a hunch that the time was come for him to drop his game of hide and seek and put all the cards in plain sight on the table. That probably was why he was coming here this morning.

Gimlet eyes that always were creeping around in search of "something!" We'd find out now what that "something" was, for it had been found—the secret of the millionaire's death had been solved. We were dead sure of that.

But it wasn't to be our luck to see the strange doctor that morning. And how we missed him, when he called at the big house, was a crazy mess, and goes to show how Fate can make a monkey out of a fellow and change his soup into sour vinegar.

There was a door to this room that we were in, with a heavy self-catch on the outside. And swung shut by the wind, which had come up with the sun and now was twisting the whole sandy countryside out of shape, we seemed to be as completely imprisoned as though our "cage" had been made of steel instead of heavy boards.

"Well, I'll be jiggered!" came Poppy's much-used expression, when he found that the door had latched itself on the outside, where we couldn't reach it.

"Phew!" I gagged, holding my nose with one hand

and feeling around in the dark with the other. "Open the ventilator—quick!"

"The 'ventilator's' closed, Jerry."

"Go on!"

"Honest. I can't budge it."

I laughed then. I thought it was a good joke on us. For I never *dreamed* that we couldn't jimmy the latch and quickly get out. But we learned in the next twenty or thirty minutes that the man who had hung this door had put it up for keeps.

Still, we *had* to get out. For having broken one of the filled bottles in kicking around in the dark, the gaggy drug smell was getting thicker every minute. We tried throwing our double weight against the door. That made it crack. Pretty soon we were panting from the hard work, with the sweat doing canal stuff down our necks. But we kept on. And finally the door went down, with the two of us sprawled on top of it like a pair of four-legged octopuses.

Cooling off for a minute or two, we ran to the house, where Ma Doane met us mysteriously at the kitchen door.

"Sh-h-h-h!" she breathed, with a finger to her thin lips.

Poppy let out his neck toward the inner rooms.

"Is the doctor here?" he inquired |eagerly, though in a careful voice.

THE GALLOPING SNAIL 183

"That's what I want to talk to you about," and the housekeeper quietly closed the doors leading into the adjoining rooms. Facing us, I saw now how big her eyes were. "I don't want your friend to hear me," she explained, meaning old Goliath, "for I find that he runs and tells everything in the sick room. And Pa isn't to know about this until to-night, so the doctor said."

"Know about what?" came quickly from Poppy.

"That all he's got is the hives and indigestion. You see, Lawyer Chew is liable to bring the sheriff here any minute to put us out. And when Dr. Madden learned of the predicament I was in, he and I together worked out a scheme to temporarily keep the lawyer away." The gray eyes sort of twinkled now. "The doctor isn't quite 'sure' about Pa's case. See? And to be safe—for it might be very contagious, you know!—he tacked up a quarantine sign on the front door. So now, if the sheriff comes, we have only to show him the sign and tell him to scoot."

"Hot dog!" laughed Poppy, thinking of how old fatty would huff and puff in his defeat. "Where is the doctor, Mrs. Doane?—upstairs?"

"Oh, he's gone."

For an instant the leader looked blank.

"Gone!" he squeaked.

"He didn't stay here more than ten or fifteen minutes."

"But we thought he had come to clear up the mystery."

"I don't think he knows half as much about this mystery as you boys imagine."

Poppy looked at me.

"Shall we tell her, Jerry?"

"I think we ought to," I waggled.

This talk stirred up the woman's curiosity.

"You boys act as though you have a secret," she leaned forward.

"Not only one," laughed Poppy, "but a whole case of 'em." Then he added, with a curious look at the woman: "Didn't your smeller put you wise to anything about the doctor, Mrs. Doane?"

"My *smeller?* What do you mean?"

"Didn't you notice that his clothes had a sort of *queer* smell?"

"No-o," came with a slow shake of her head.

"And you didn't smell anything on him that made you think of—of something else?"

The same answer was given.

"What do you know about Dr. Madden," the question was then put to us, "that you should speak of him so queerly?"

But Poppy wasn't ready to answer that yet.

"And you're positive," he hung on, "that the doctor's clothes didn't have a queer smell?—a sort of *drug-store* smell?"

"I didn't put my nose *on* him," came stiffly, "but I smelt nothing when I stood beside him."

Poppy dropped that point.

"All right. We'll take it for granted that he had on other clothes. . . Did he say anything about the granddaughter?"

"Yes. I think he was disappointed not to find her here."

The leader gave me a quick wink.

"But if he and the girl aren't mixed up together, as I told you last night, how did he know she was coming here? You say it's a secret."

"Why! . ." the woman stared. "I hadn't thought of that."

"You say he was disappointed not to find the granddaughter here," Poppy went on. "Do you mean he was *surprised?*"

"Ye-es. He acted both surprised and disappointed —almost troubled, in fact. And from words that he dropped offhand I got the impression that he wanted to talk with her about something important. I told him that so far as we knew she was hiding in Pardyville. And thinking I might corner him, and thus prove the truth of your theory, I says: 'Possibly, Doctor, you know *where* she is hiding.' But all I got was a stare of surprise. 'I wish,' says he earnestly, 'that I did know where she is. For it is very important that we find her to-day. And taking your tip, I shall drive over to Pardyville myself and see if I can locate her.' Then we put up the quarantine sign and he drove away."

Poppy wasn't so sure of himself now.

"And you really believe, Mrs. Doane," says he, puzzled, "that the doctor is dumb on where the girl is?"

"Remembering his earnest words and actions, I cannot doubt it for a moment."

We then told the woman about our discovery in the barn. And while we were talking, the sound of hoofs and steel buggy wheels came to us from the graveled drive, as on the preceding day. Running to the front door, we got a glimpse of young fatty, driving his father's rig, while on the small half of the seat sat a tall, rangy man with a mean-looking star pinned on his vest.

CHAPTER XVIII

A WHISPERING VOICE

"It's Lawyer Chew's rig," says Mrs. Doane, with a puzzled look at the newcomers.

"Yes," says Poppy, "and the sort of near-human-looking object that you see squashed on the seat behind the whip socket is Lawyer Chew's pet son, Eggbert."

"He looks like his father."

"And *acts* like him, too, you'll find."

It didn't take young fatty as long to untangle himself from the buggy seat as his old man. And, say, did he ever strut it off as he came toward the house! The king had arrived! You tell 'em! And now, at a snap of his royal fingers, everybody and everything in the landscape, not on his side, would do a neat and obedient little loop-the-loop.

Yah, he had us licked in his own mind even before he got out of his pa's spraddle-wheeled buggy. But don't weep too soon over our sad fate. For you may find that there's a laugh coming yet.

Chuckling, Poppy pulled me back out of sight.

"Quick, Jerry!—to the kitchen."

"What for?"

"To find a pail."

"What kind of a pail?"

"Any kind," came the giggle, "just so long as it holds water. And the more water the better."

"Hot dog!" says I, seeing fun ahead. "Are you going to give young fatty a shower bath?"

"Nothing else but."

In a jiffy we had a pail. Not a skinny one, either, but a sort of robust, full-grown pail. Just fatty's size. And filling it with cold water, we hoisted it up the stairs, for it was the leader's scheme to do the "showering" act through an upper window.

So that we would be completely out of sight, we went clear up to the third floor. Nor did our window give us away with any squeaky stuff when he guardedly opened it.

"Reserved seats," grinned the leader, rubbering over the sill.

Below us, the over-fed rooster was still doing his cock-a-doodle-doo stuff.

"My name's Chew," we heard him give out importantly in front of Mrs. Doane. "I guess you know who my father is, for he was here yesterday."

"Yes," says the little old lady calmly, "I know a great deal about your father. And I knew your *grandfather*, too, whom you resemble, *in your actions*,

THE GALLOPING SNAIL 189

a great deal more than you probably realize."

But fatty didn't get that.

"My father has me help him, so that I can learn the business," came importantly. "And he sent me over here to lock up this place, and see that it is kept locked up."

"Was he *afraid* to come himself?"

"Afraid? Of *you?*" and the fat smart aleck gave the meanest laugh you can imagine. Boy, he sure was trying to act hard-boiled! "No," came the further strut, "he wasn't *afraid*. He had other business that was more important. . . You've got just ten minutes to get your stuff packed. And if you aren't ready to beat it then, the sheriff here will do a clever little trick to help you along. Savvy?"

This brought the man forward.

"The boy's a bit blunt, ma'am," came in a not unkindly voice. "Yet he has stated the case correctly. Unless you promptly leave here of your own accord, I'll have to serve the papers on you that were given to me for that purpose."

"I suppose," says Mrs. Doane stiffly, "that in planning to move us out of here, you even brought along an ambulance stretcher."

"An ambulance stretcher? What for?"

"My husband is sick in bed. We had the doctor for him this morning. And while it probably isn't a case of *smallpox*, still the doctor thought it would be wise to put up a quarantine sign. You might not have noticed it."

"I swan!" exclaimed the man, getting his eyes on the sign. Then he turned to the kid. "Guess, Sonny, this changes things considerable."

"It's a trick!" danced young fatty. "Don't let her fool you."

After a look at puggy-nose, which showed plainly enough what she thought of him, the woman turned to the officer.

"There's a 'phone in the house," says she. "And if you wish, you can call up Dr. Madden of Neponset Corners and verify my story. Or," dryly, "if you care to run the risk, you can go up to the sick room and see the invalid for yourself. But if he coaxes you to scratch the purple blotches on his back, please don't do it. For, as I just told you, it may be catching."

The man was eager enough to get away.

"Your word's good with me, ma'am," says he, backing off.

But bulldog-face wasn't going to give up his bone without a scrap.

"Dumb-bell!" he screeched. "Don't you know your onions? It's a trick, I tell you. And if you don't call her bluff, and put her out of here, my father'll fix you."

THE GALLOPING SNAIL

The man didn't like that, but he hung onto his temper.

"Servin' papers on smallpox cases hain't in my line, Sonny," says he quietly.

"Smallpox, your granny! . . I'm going in and 'phone, if you don't."

"Help yourself," drawled the officer, giving the kid the same kind of a look that Mrs. Doane had.

Fatty had talked brave. But he backed down now. For it suddenly percolated into his thick skull, I guess, that the woman might be telling the truth, after all. Anyway, he didn't go inside to use the telephone.

The sheriff had gone back to the buggy, as though the morning's work was over so far as he was concerned. This gave us the very chance we were looking for. But as I grabbed the pail of water, to heave it out of the window in good aim, Poppy stopped me.

"Look, Jerry!"

He was pointing to the eaves over our heads. And what do you know if there wasn't a hornets' nest up there, under the roof edge, as big as a tub. It had more holes in it than Red Meyers has freckles, and there was a pa and ma hornet and nine frisky little hornets with brand new stingers and sassy tempers for every hole. Boy, were we ever in luck!

Down below, fatty was spreading around some

more of his mean gab. His father would see about *this* and his father would see about *that*. Quarantine sign or no quarantine sign, his father would blub-blub-blub-blub!

Poppy slid the stick out of the bottom part of the window shade.

"Get ready, Jerry. When I count 'three,' dump your bucket. And at the same time I'll poke the nest loose."

The sheriff had his eyes on us now. But though he saw what we were doing, he didn't give us away. It tickled him, I guess, to see smarty get it in the neck.

"One, two, *three*," says Poppy, and down went the water and the hornets, only the water, being the heaviest, hit the fat target first. Doused from head to foot, young fatty gave a gurgle like a staggering bull when the nest pancaked on his dome. He knew, of course, that it was a trick. And looking up to see where the water and nest had come from, he found twenty-seven million homeless hornets swooping down at him in vengeance. One old gladiator, who could pump his wings faster than the others, made a swish with his sword, ramming it clear through the upturned pug nose. Then, boy, oh, boy, did hunky ever howl! He took to his heels, swinging his arms over his bean like a drunken windmill. But he wasn't

HE TOOK TO HIS HEELS AS TWENTY-SEVEN MILLION HORNETS SWOOPED DOWN AT HIM.

Poppy Ott and the Galloping Snail.   *Page* 192

THE GALLOPING SNAIL 193

fast enough to get away from another old lunker, who stabbed him six inches deep in the tight part of his pants. With one great and mighty howl, the runner jumped clear over a nine-foot bush. Anyway, it was a bush.

Closing the window, we scooted downstairs.

"Laws-a-me!" laughed Mrs. Doane, getting her eyes on our empty pail. "Was it you boys who threw the water? I never saw anything so funny, and so *appropriate*, in all my life. And those *hornets!*" Then, grimly: "My only regret is that it wasn't Lawyer Chew, himself, who got it, instead of his son."

It was going to eleven o'clock now. We had dinner an hour later, then Poppy and I fixed up the door in the barn as best we could, for we had no right to smash it down and go off and leave it that way.

We did a lot of talking back and forth as we worked. But I don't know as I need to write it all down. You know everything that we knew. And probably the things that puzzled us are puzzling you. It was a big disappointment to us that we had missed seeing Dr. Madden. In spite of our discoveries in the barn, Mrs. Doane didn't believe that he was deep in the mystery. But we did. It wasn't anything that he hadn't smelt druggy when he made his morning call. Clean clothes and a bath could have fixed him up O. K. As for acting worried over the "lost" granddaughter, that could have all been put on. Or even if he *didn't* know where she was, that in no way left him out of the tangle. Not by a long shot. Wherever the girl was, or whatever her secret ideas were in hiding—on him, possibly, as well as on the rest of us—he had yet to tell *why* he had hid himself in the closed house for a whole year.

He would be back in the evening, he had told Mrs. Doane. Sure thing, he would be back! Just as Poppy had said in dishing out his theory, it was the hider's scheme, in having solved the mystery of the millionaire's death, to spring a surprise when the will was read. So now, as you can imagine, we were crazy for night to come. For we wanted to find out *why* the dead man's loyal friend had hid in the lonely house, with queer-smelling drugs all around him, and what he had uncovered.

Poppy took it into his head to do some more sleuthing in the upper rooms, hopeful, I guess, that he would pick up a clew in the way of a cuff link, or something like that, as usually happens in detective stories. I saw that he didn't need me, and going downstairs to help Mrs. Doane, who was sweeping and dusting for dear life, so that everything in the house would be spick and span for the big party that night, I found her at the telephone.

"What? I can't hear a word you say." She jiggled the receiver hook. "Speak louder, please. What? Dr. Madden? What did you say? Dr. Madden *what?* . . No, all I can hear is 'Dr. Madden.' Just a minute," and trembling like a leaf, she partly turned and motioned to me. "There's a boy here, and I'll let him talk. Maybe he has sharper ears than me."

The receiver switched hands.

"It's long distance," she told me nervously. "And I *think* it's Pardyville, but I'm not certain. Oh, dear! How helpless people do get when they grow old. I hope it isn't bad news. If the call *is* from Pardyville, no doubt the doctor has found Miss Ruth. And certainly *that* isn't bad news."

"Hello," says I, jamming the receiver against one ear and prodding a finger into the other, as I had seen Dad do on long-distance calls. "Who's speaking?"

"This is the St. Elizabeth hospital at Pardyville," came a faint distant voice. "Can you hear me?"

"Yes," says I.

A hospital! That wasn't a very favorable start, I thought, for good news. We never had *dreamed* that the granddaughter, in getting into some kind of a possible accident, had been taken to a hospital.

"We have an accident case here—Dr. Madden of Neponset Corners. Do you know him?"

"Yes," says I, with my heart thumping.

"His automobile turned turtle a mile outside of town, and he is quite seriously injured. Knowing that he might not survive the operation, he wants to talk with Mrs. Ivor Doane. It must be important, for he insists on doing the talking himself, though he is in a very weakened condition. Is Mrs. Doane there?"

"I'm taking the message for her," I explained.

"Then listen carefully."

There was a metal-like click at the other end of the wire; then a short deep silence. My heart was pounding. I don't think I ever was more excited in all my life. Realizing that he was done for, the queer doctor was going to make a confession that would clear up the mystery. I was going to hear strange things. But I didn't let my excitement tangle up my wits. I needed a clear brain now. I realized that.

"This is—Dr. Madden," came a whispering voice over the wire.

"Yes?" says I, sort of breathless-like.

"Tell Mrs. Doane—that Ruth Danver will lose—her grandfather's property—if she isn't in the house—before midnight—to-night. Diary in clock—explains everything. I found it—and hid it there. Do you—hear me?"

THE GALLOPING SNAIL 197

"Yes," says I.

"The clock—in Mr. Danver's room. Do you understand?"

"Yes," says I.

There was a dead silence then. The whispering voice was gone. And I knew what that meant. Without getting a chance to be operated on, the man was gone, too.

I started to shiver. I don't know why, unless it was like having a man die in front of me, sort of. Things like that get the best of a boy. But after a minute or two I was all right again. I told Mrs. Doane about the accident and the whispering voice. Then we ran upstairs to find Poppy and get the diary out of the clock.

CHAPTER XIX

THE DIARY IN THE CLOCK

WE found Poppy in the big bedroom, doing detective stuff with a yardstick. But whatever his job was, he dropped the work in a hurry when I told him about the whispering voice on the telephone.

Everything was dark inside of the big floor clock. So we got the flashlight, which was working again, the leader having cleverly touched it up. The light helping us to see, we found a leather-covered book in the very bottom of the clock, sort of tucked away in a dark corner. It had D-I-A-R-Y printed on it in gold letters, and under the printing was the dead man's name.

"Corbin Danver's diary!" cried Mrs. Doane, acting as though she was afraid to touch the book. "Is it right for us to read it?" she held off, in her nervous way.

"From what Jerry tells us," says Poppy, "I take it that we've *got* to read it. For if Miss Ruth is liable to lose out on getting this property, as Dr. Madden said, we want to help her—that really was his idea in calling us up. And how can we help her unless we know what the mix-up is all about?"

That was talking horse sense, all right. So we took the diary to the window, for better light, and got busy on it, finding that it went back more than twenty years.

The most of the writing, we found out, in skimming through the book, was sort of unimportant. So, instead of telling you everything, word for word, I'll pick out just the *mystery* stuff.

Stopping in Africa on a trip around the world, a traveling companion of the millionaire's had picked up a fatal jungle disease, like leprosy, and had been buried there.

"I find myself wondering," the rich man wrote in his book, "if I, too, might not contract this fulsome disease. Poor Travis! Would that I had been able to trek his body back to civilization. . . I shall watch my hands carefully for any sign of those fatal white blotches."

Then, shortly after the globe trotter had come back to America:

"In Boston I met Dr. Arthur Madden, as fine a young gentleman, and as ardent a scholar in his chosen work, as was his father before him, than whom I probably never will have a dearer or more trustworthy friend. Out of medical college less than a year, young Madden is specializing in diseases of the skin and flesh. So, thinking it might interest him, I told him the story of poor Travis. Readily placing the disease in his mental catalog of human ailments, domestic and foreign, and much concerned over the fact that I had been over the same ground with Travis, he examined my hands so searchingly as to first make me nervous. But when he asked to see my *feet*, my native humor asserted itself. More than a year having passed since Travis' death, does this young scholar imagine that I still am liable to come down with the disease? He talked so learnedly of *latent germs*, that I was inwardly amused, the more so as I contrasted his rather flowery science with that of his father, a staid practitioner of the older school of medicine."

We skipped two years here.

"I had a letter to-day from young Madden, who has buried himself (along with his germs!) in a little country town by the name of Neponset Corners. In his research work, he is eager to build a country sanitarium, for patients of 'incurable' skin diseases. This letter, I fancy, is somewhat of an invitation for me to back his scheme financially. Well, I shall see what the young man is doing down there when I visit him next month, as he has urged me to do. Lately I haven't been feeling at my best, and I shall enjoy the quiet of the country."

A skip of two months.

"These have been hours of the deepest mental torture to me. Nor has Madden incorrectly diagnosed my case, as I had so hoped in the beginning. The white blotches on my right leg, that meant nothing to me when I first came here, have daily become more pronounced."

Another skip.

"I feel that I owe my life to Madden. There can be no doubt of the miracle that his drugs have worked in me. My end is not to be as tragic as poor Travis'! Madden's faith in germs is more profound than ever. My malady is under medical control, he tells me, but the *germs* are still in my system, as they have been since Travis and I were simultaneously infected in the jungle. They may forever lie dormant in my blood vessels, if I keep myself physically fit, as I was abroad. Yet to-morrow, if I let myself run down, they may take a deadly grip on me. Of necessity, I shall remain very close to this good friend of mine, so that he may ever be quickly available, in case I need him, which, of course, I pray that I shall not. Then, too, he is not without hope that a drug may be compounded that will completely exterminate the germs. So, as anxious as I am to remain here, it also is something of a duty to science for me to stay."

A skip of three years here.

"My son, Harold, is quite incensed over this country building project of mine. It is his fear, I think, that I am getting childish, and thus proving incapable of managing my own affairs. Yet, could he but know the truth, how different would be his attitude toward me! I feel, though, that the isolation that the country place will afford is highly advisable, notwithstanding the fact that Madden has repeatedly assured me that the communication of this disease, except at its native source, is possibly only through blood transfusion. How fortunate that I am not a peril to those around me! Yet, even so, I shrink from having my malady known. And having pressed Madden to secrecy, it is my plan to keep even my own son in ignorance of my condition until I can go to him completely cured. . . This place that I am planning to build is going to cost heavily. But in the three years and more that I have been living here with Madden, both to my own welfare and in the possible interests of science, the money from my wide investments has been accumulating far beyond my ability to use it. So it is well, all things considered, that I proceed with my plans."

Another skip of two months.

"It seems that my recent purchase of the sandy tract north of the river, where extensive building operations are already under way, has earned for me the local reputation of being 'cracked!' Yet I smile at these stories. Only Madden and I know the truth! Harold, I understand, has a baby girl. But he has not written to me. I rather prefer, though, to have our quarrel stand. And to that point I dare say my daughter-in-law, after what I purposely said to her, will forever bear me malice, that being her nature."

A skip of a month.

"My granddaughter's name is Ruth Louise. I find myself longing to see this new mite of humanity, in whom, some day, will be vested the combined fortunes of our entire household."

A skip of two years.

"At last I am in my new home. And knowing how advisable is the isolation, very peaceful and contented I find myself here. Yet, to that point, what do I lack to complete my earthly happiness, unless, possibly, reconciliation with my son and his family? I have, I think, a very beautiful and not ordinary home here; nor have I neglected the immediate surroundings. As I look down from my window, my eyes are greeted by a gorgeous growth of foliage that almost would do credit to the tropics. What wonders fertilization and re-soiling have worked here! The results far outweigh the expense. Madden still dreams of his sanitarium. And what more suitable place than this! My remaining years may not be many, and he is still a comparatively young man. I can understand his great joy to learn, by the terms of my will, that this mammoth place (a 'white elephant,' Harold calls it) will be placed at his disposal . . . I owe it to him."

A skip of five years.

"Kept in bed by a return of the dreaded symptoms, I was unable this week to attend my son's funeral in Minneapolis, and thus, no doubt, am further estranged from my unbending and now independently-wealthy daughter-in-law. Would, though, that the granddaughter might take a less harsh view of me."

Another skip of five years.

"This has been an amazingly joyful week. My granddaughter has been here—not, however, with her mother's consent or even to her mother's knowledge! What a wonderful child Ruth is, and how great will be my joy to make her my heir. In this house of an 'an old man's fancy,' I showed her to-day the hidden staircase behind the moon. She calls this desert home of mine 'Aladdin's Palace,' though innocently dropping a remark the while to the effect that her mother calls it the 'Ogre's Den.' So I am an 'ogre' in the eyes of my daughter-in-law! Ruth undoubtedly has had to unlearn a lot of things about me in the few days that she has been here.

And she admits now that it was largely curiosity to see the 'ogre' that brought her here. Her evident affection for me, as she has come to really know me, is a joy beyond words. To-morrow she goes on to visit my cousin Samantha Doane, where she is supposed to have been during the past week. May it be that Samantha, good woman that she is, does not implant in the younger mind the seed of too vigorous conversation."

"Laws-a-me!" burst out Mrs. Doane, looking at us in turn with her big eyes. "What does he mean? —that I talk too much?"

Poppy grinned, but didn't answer.

"Again taken to my bed," the millionaire wrote, shortly before his death, "I have repeatedly tried to get in touch with my granddaughter, through Alonzo Chew, my lawyer, but she pays no attention to my letters and telegrams. Is this the work of her mother? I have tried to believe so. Yet the child, with a mind of her own, found a way of coming here last summer. So common sense tells me that she could write to me if she wished. Can it be true, as Chew says, that all she came for a year ago was to fawn on a senile old man and thus insure her heritage? She wants my money, he says, and getting it, less than ever will she want to come to this isolated home of mine. Chew is wiring her again to-day, that

I am on my deathbed, and that may bring her. We had another long talk when he was here about those poor people in the religious colony by the river. I was surprised at his deep interest in them, and his evident desire to help them to happier homes and more productive surroundings. Rather than have my wealth dissipated by a thankless younger relative, how much finer, he has urged, that I might invest it in the lives of these deserving people. I could do for them, on their rather barren land, what I had done for myself here. And the result, in their greater happiness and added prosperity, would be a lasting monument to my memory. I find myself so easily led on by Chew, that I wonder at times, and anxiously, if my mind is inhabited by its usual keenness. . . To think that I should even consider disinheriting my own grandchild!"

A skip of two days.

"Still not a line from Ruth. And this indifference of hers, so heart-breaking to me, has led to the making of a new will, though it isn't the will that Chew tried to urge on me. But I cannot bring myself to disinherit my kin outright. Maybe, when I am gone, Ruth will be filled with remorse over her present conduct. And how tragic then that my fortune should have passed into strange hands! No, I have let the disposition of my property stand for a year. And I can only hope that my grandchild, in getting the keys of my home, as I intend sending them to her through Dr. Madden, will understand that I *want* her to come here. If she does come, any time within a year after I am gone—and she has until midnight of the last day—then the entire estate will be hers, with the exception of this place, which I want Dr. Madden to have, along with the necessary endowment. If she doesn't come, proof to me that she has no happy recollection of the hours that she spent here, the bulk of the estate will be left as a religious trust fund, the money to be disbursed locally by Chew as he sees fit."

The diary ended here. It had taken us about two hours to go through it, though it hasn't taken you ten minutes to read what we picked out—only we didn't write it down at the time: I borrowed the diary and did that afterwards.

We knew now *why* the big house had been built here, a secret in itself, and *why* the body had smelt of drugs. Every part of the dead man's secret was spread out in our understanding minds. We saw into the lawyer's scheme, too. He hadn't written to the granddaughter, at all. And probably he had done everything he could to keep her away from the closed-up house until the year was up. A lot of religious interest *he* had in the New Zion gang! If they got anything at all out of the fortune, it would be pennies that slipped through his greedy fingers. In the diary, Mr. Danver had said something about his head being on the bum. It sure had been on the bum, all right, to make a will like *that!*

Oh, if only we could knock the props out from under old fatty! It was an awful thought that he was liable to win out. It fairly made us sick. But what could we do? Certainly, it was too late to go to Pardyville, even if we had known for sure that the granddaughter was hiding there.

Another thing that put weight on our gloom was Dr. Madden's death. We had figured on him doing something to-night to help the granddaughter. Now he was gone. And unless he had made a further confession at the hospital, before I talked with him, we might never know *why* he had been hiding in the closed-up house.

That he had "found" the diary, proved, though, even more than the box of drugs in the barn, that he *had* been hiding here. Reading the book, and thus getting wise to old Chew's dishonest scheme, he had sent for the granddaughter, who, in turn, had written to the two Doanes, asking them to come on ahead and open up the place for her.

But why had the "druggy" hider slammed the door so mysteriously? Where did the gander come in? And why had the granddaughter dropped out of *his* sight as well as everybody else's? Finally, and most important of all, where was she?

CHAPTER XX

"MISS" POPPY OTT

YES, sir, the more we messed the matter around in our minds the more we were made to realize how very little Dr. Madden had told on himself. His secrets were still shut up. And, "man of mystery" that he was, the only reason why he had told us about the hidden diary was to give the granddaughter a square deal. Knocked out himself, he wanted us to help her, if we could, and thus defeat the scheming lawyer.

That old hunk of human fat! How we hated him! We wanted to trim him to a frazzle. But how were we going to do it? It looked kind of hopeless.

But Poppy isn't the kind of a kid to give up without a struggle. I guess not. And it was his gritty scheme now to waylay the lawyer, when he came that night, and lock him up in the barn. If necessary, we would keep the human lard-pail shut up for several days, which would give us a chance to look around for the granddaughter. Then, if we found her, we would turn him loose, and she could stare at him in surprise and say: "Well, old hunk, where have *you* been all summer?" Do you catch on? Having been shut up in the barn, he wouldn't be able to *prove* that she hadn't tripped into the house in time to save her fortune. A kind of tricky scheme, it's true, but look who we were fighting!

Ma, poor old soul, seemed sort of shrunken over the fact that the red-plush settee hadn't been mentioned in the diary. She *just knew* that she wasn't going to get it. Or, worse, she might not get anything at all! Never having heard people talk so open and frank-like about such things, it was kind of funny to us. But, bu-lieve me, we got the grin out of our eyes in a hurry when the wilted little old lady began to cry. We saw then how much the settee meant to her. And realizing that she might get left out, after all, we wondered if we couldn't buy the piece for her. We still had sixteen dollars.

To our surprise, young fatty breezed in just before supper, having brought another doctor—a tall, willowy geezer with mutton-chop whiskers and a jug-handle nose. And speaking of noses, I wish you could have seen squashy's bugle. It was all over his face. Like a big toadstool. And when he walked he sort of *spraddled*.

"Where was the wreck?" grinned Poppy.

That made the kid furious. For he knew, of course, who had sicked the hornets on him.

"I'll 'wreck' you," he fired at us, "if you don't crawl into a hole and shut up."

Crawl into a hole for *him?* Oh, yes! We'd even pull the hole in after us, if he said so. Like so much mud!

Knowing his stuff, the new doctor soon found out the truth about old Ivory Dome's hives, and, in consequence, down came the quarantine sign. It was fatty, of course, who yanked the sign down. But he met with a snag when he tried to call the sheriff back. For the country officer wasn't at home.

"Just the same," the fat hunk blustered around, as mean as mud, "you've got to git out of here— every last one of you."

Poppy had stood about enough.

"And suppose we don't get out," says he, kind of screwing his eyes down to little black spots, "are you going to *put* us out?"

Fatty saw that he was heading into trouble.

"My father will," he blustered.

"With a posse, huh?"

"It won't take much to put *you* out," was slung across the room, as the fat one's temper got away from him.

"No?" purred Poppy. "Would you like to try it . . . yourself?"

"Two against one," came the sneer.

THE GALLOPING SNAIL

Never have I known a kid who can hold his temper any better than Poppy. And what the steady leader did now, instead of soaking the fat smart aleck, was to give me a wink.

"Get a tapeline, Jerry."

"What for?" says I.

"We're going to do some measuring."

I caught on then, for once before we had pulled this stunt of making a monkey out of the other guy. And perfectly suited with the program, I borrowed a tape measure from the housekeeper and got busy.

"Five feet six," says I, giving fatty's height.

Poppy gravely wrote that down.

"Twenty-eight inches from starboard to poop deck," says I, meaning across the hips.

That was written down, too.

"Eighteen inches under the cover," says I.

The writer looked at me.

"Does that allow room on the breast for a wreath of calla lilies?" he inquired solemnly.

"Maybe you better make it twenty inches," I corrected, not wanting to crush the funeral boquet.

Fatty got away from me then.

"Don't git fresh," says he, scowling, "or you'll find yourself playing a harp."

Poppy held his pencil ready.

"How many handles do you want on it?" says he.

"I'll put a 'handle' on your nose, **if you** don't shut up."

"Like your own, huh?" I put in.

"Three handles on a side is the usual plan," says the writer thoughtfully. "But maybe I better make it four on a side for *you*. . . East and west or north and south?"

Old thick-skull wasn't traveling fast enough for us now.

"I mean," the writer explained patiently, "do you want us to dig the grave so it'll lay east and west or north and south?"

"Grave? Whose grave?"

"*Good* night!" I yipped. "You sure are dumb. What did you think we were measuring you up for? —a new dress suit?"

"Go lay an egg," says fatty.

"And here's a nice little epitaph to go on the tombstone," says Poppy:

> Once I was fat and sassy—
> The village shiek in my day—
> Then I got too blamed brassy
> And they tenderly laid me away—with a brick.

"I'll 'lay' you away!"

Poppy suddenly dropped his game.

"The point is, kid, that we're harder than nails. Our middle name is dynamite. When we hits 'em, they lay. And while this may be a disappointment to you, I'll have to tell you outright that we don't intend to move out of here to-night. So, if you want to stay here, yourself, the less you blow around about putting us out, the better it will be for you. Do you git me?"

The doctor driving away, Ma called us to supper, and what do you know if fatty didn't have the nerve to park himself at the table along with the rest of us!

"It's his scheme," says Poppy, when we were outside, "to wait here for his old man."

"He'll have a long wait," I laughed, thinking of how we were going to coop up the fat lawyer in the bottle room.

"Maybe we ought to lock the kid up, too," came thoughtfully. "Then he won't be able to give us away."

I caught on. With the kid in the house, we couldn't very well let on afterwards that the granddaughter had been there when it was known to him that she wasn't. Yet I didn't like the idea of locking him up. Too much of this "locking-up" stuff would get us into trouble.

"Say, Poppy," I laughed, as a crazy idea began to stagger around in my head. "Do you want to do the trick up right?"

"It's a cinch," came earnestly, "that I don't want to fumble."

"Then listen to this," I laughed again, more eager to further make a monkey of fatty than to jump on him. "We catch old law-book and lock him up. Then, having drawn cuts, the short-straw fellow is the 'she.'"

"'She?' What she?"

"The granddaughter."

I had him puzzled.

"For example," I went on, "we'll suppose that you're the 'she.' And having borrowed one of Ma Doane's petticoats, we dress you up in it. Then, just before midnight the 'granddaughter' trips in. Kisses and hugs at the front door. 'Ruthie, dearest, I'm *so* glad to see you—and did you have a pleasant journey, my love?' Fatty is there, taking it all in. But gloom and disappointment for him. Do you catch on?"

"Jerry, you're cuckoo."

"Cuckoo, nothing," I hung on, seeing the fun that we could have.

"Not me," he held off.

"What are you scared of?"

"I'd feel cute dressed up like a girl!"

"It'll be a scream."

"Yah—for you!"

I was grinning more than ever.

"When you flutter in, kid, looking like Mary Pickford on her wedding day, I'll meet you at the door and give you an old smacker right on the two-lip bed."

"It won't work, Jerry. For I'm too bow-legged to pass for a girl."

"Say, what do you think we're going to pull off?—a bathing-beauty contest?'

"It would be a *side-show* if you had your way about it."

"Suppose your legs *are* sort of corkscrewed," says I, looking him over. "Your petticoat will cover that up."

His eyes were dancing now. For big monkey that he is, he's as full of crazy fun as the next fellow.

"I get to fix the straws, huh?"

"Sure thing—if you don't cheat."

The straws fixed, I drew first, hopeful that I would be luckier than the other time in the barn.

"Mine's the shortest," the other tried to snudge.

"Like so much mud!" I yipped happily.

Running into the house, we quickly told the little old lady about our scheme.

"What nonsense!" she sputtered.

"But if we don't do it, Mrs. Doane," I hung on, "how are we going to pretend afterwards that the girl was here before midnight?"

"Oh, dear! I don't want Miss Ruth to lose her fortune. Even if I get nothing myself—and I noticed several odd dishes in the cupboard just like my company set—I don't want Lawyer Chew to walk off with everything."

"Of course not," says I quickly. "So any scheme to help the granddaughter is worth trying."

"I hardly know what to say. For after the way things have been stirred up here, I haven't confidence in my judgment any more."

"Which means 'yes,' huh?"

"But can you really do it?" came doubtfully.

"Leave it to old Poppy," I bragged, slapping my chum on the back. "He's clever."

"I won't feel clever," the other suffered in advance, "with petticoats on."

"You'll make a swell flapper," I stepped around.

Oh, boy, I kept thinking to myself, wasn't I the lucky little thing that it wasn't me.

He gritted his teeth.

"Jerry, if you ever tell about this at home! . . . Gr-r-r-r!"

Cornering old Goliath, whose hair, you'll remember, hung to his shoulders, we got busy on him with a pair of shears. He didn't mind. When we got through with him he looked like a bald-headed convict.

THE GALLOPING SNAIL 219

Working in the closed room, Ma's fingers flew as she took the hair as we clipped it and made it into a wig. As a sort of rehearsal, I privately helped Poppy into the outfit—and standing there in the middle of the room, did he ever look like a whipped puppy! First came slippers and long silk stockings. Then a fancy petticoat of Ma's. And over that a hand-worked dress that the elder, fortunately, had brought along as a present for the younger relative. With the wig on, and his eyebrows touched up with a burnt match, "Miss" Poppy Ott was the snappiest little chicken that ever cracked a shiek's heart.

Ma came back to the room.

"I swan!" she told Poppy. "You look more like a girl than Miss Ruth, herself. For, if the truth is known, *she* always acted like a tomboy."

Poppy wiggled.

"It's too tight," he suffered at the waist.

"You don't want to look like a tub," I stood off and admired him.

"I feel like a fool," he grunted.

"Nix on the bass-drum talk," says I. "Squeak."

"What do you think I am?—a rusty hinge?"

"Make your voice sound like a girl's."

He puckered up gamely.

"And do I sound like a girl now?" he squeaked.

"You'll do, Poppy," I slapped him on the back. "Gee, kid, you're clever."

"Remember," he glared at me, as he powdered his nose, "one word of this when we get home, and your folks will pick you up with a blotter."

We were all set now. And as it was getting close to nine o'clock, we took old Goliath with us and went out to the front gate, where we tied a rope from pillar to pillar.

"The trick is," Poppy explained to the giant, "that we've got to stop old Chew from going into the house. And being big and husky, we brought you along to help us."

"Sure thing," waggled old baldy. "What do you want me to do?—wring his neck?"

"He deserves it," grinned the leader, "but I guess we hadn't better do that. For it might get us into trouble with the law. A safer plan will be to lock him up in the barn."

Pretty soon the lawyer came along, having learned from his smart son, of course, that the quarantine sign was a trick.

"Gid-dap!" the driver flopped the lines, when the horse stopped at the gate. But the old nag never budged. Grumbling, the big one got out to see what was wrong, which gave us a chance to tackle him, football style, after which Goliath lugged him off to the barn.

THE GALLOPING SNAIL

With the horse and buggy out of sight, we ran back to the kitchen, where we found young fatty helping himself to one of Ma Doane's choice apple pies. The big pig! Poppy and I had spotted that particular pie for ourselves.

The door-bell ringing at eleven-thirty, the fat kid beat it into the hall, sure now, after an uneasy hour, that his father had finally arrived to do the will reading.

"Why," came a familiar squeaky voice from the open door, "if it isn't little *Egg*bert!"

Now, I'll admit right off the bat that this "girl" stuff of ours was a crazy mess. We probably shouldn't have done it. Certainly, it didn't get us anything in the end. But, even so, before I go any farther, I think I ought to hand old Poppy a hunk of praise. For he sure was carrying out his part to perfection. Not only did he *look* like a girl, but he acted like one. His voice was a bit off-key, of course. But that was nothing.

"Miss Ruth!" cried the housekeeper, playing her part. "Miss Ruth has come at last!"

CHAPTER XXI

BEHIND THE MOON

WELL, with all of Poppy's cleverness, the wonder to me is, as I look back, that fatty was fooled. For he wasn't a dumb-bell. Yet, to our good luck, he never caught on. And if ever you saw a disappointed face it was his, which showed plainly enough that he knew how the will read.

Mrs. Doane was buzzing around like a bumblebee. It was "dearie this" and "dearie that." And when "dearie," in walking up and down the room, got out a compact and powdered "her" nose, I thought I'd die. Everything looked *so* natural, "she" purred— only it was more of a squeak than a purr.

Having tried without success to get his mother on the telephone, young fatty primped in front of the hall mirror, to make himself pretty, and then sidled up to the "heiress" on the sofa.

"How did you know it was me?" he blushed.

"Oh! . . . I'm a mind reader," and the sick-calf look that the "heiress" gave him out of the corner of "her" eyes almost turned my stomach. But fatty thought it was sugar and cream.

THE GALLOPING SNAIL 223

"Are you going to be here very long?" he inquired eagerly.

"Pos-sibly."

"Say, can I—I— I mean," it finally tumbled out, "can I have a date some night soon?"

"I'd love to, if—"

"If what?"

"If your mama will let you."

"Huh! I don't have to ask *her* to go out on a date."

"No-o?"

"I'm sixteen."

"*Sweet* sixteen."

"Gee!" says fatty, in clover.

"I suppose you'll be getting married . . . soon."

"I guess I'd marry you, all right," the fortune hunter blurted out, "if I had a chance."

"Silly!"

"It's funny my father doesn't come."

"Hasn't he been here at all to-night?"

"No."

"And grandpa's will hasn't been read?"

"No. . . . Say, you won't forget, will you?"

"About the date?"

"Sure thing."

"Oh! . . . I'll never forget *that*."

"And you know what you said," reminded the fast worker.

"What?"

"About me—me— You know."

"Getting married?"

"Sure thing. Maybe we will, some day."

"Little me and little you?"

"I guess you're making fun of me now."

"How could I?"

"I'm not little."

"I think you're cute. . . . Does your nose always look that way?"

"A hornet stung me."

"You poor dear! If Aunty wasn't looking, I'd kiss it for you."

Fatty almost fell off the sofa.

"Say—" he gurgled. "Say— Let's go out and sit in the hall."

"Would you try to kiss me in the dark?"

"I would if I got a chance."

"When you're with the girl you love, you want to be *brave* and take a chance."

"Say, you aren't like most girls."

"I know that, all right."

"But I like you the better for it."

"You might not like me so well, if you knew *everything*."

THE GALLOPING SNAIL

"Have you got another fellow?" came hastily.

"Oh, no! You're the only lover I ever had."

"I *do* love you."

"Of course."

"There's something about your voice that seems familiar to me."

"I probably whispered to you in your dreams."

"I'll dream about you to-night, all right."

"You might not, if you knew *everything*."

"Why do you keep saying that?"

"Oh, I just want to tease you. . . . There, the clock struck midnight."

"I guess you're lucky."

"In having you for a . . friend?"

"Yes . . . sure thing. But that isn't what I meant."

"No-o?"

"You're lucky that you got here just when you did."

"Why?"

"Don't you know about the will?"

"Grandpa's will?"

"Sure thing. He was going to cut you off if you hadn't got here before midnight. I heard my father tell my mother."

"And now . . . what do I get?"

"Everything."

"And what do *you* get?"

"Nothing."

"But you've got *me*."

"I wish we were older."

"Why?"

"We'd get married right away."

"And my money would be your money, wouldn't it?"

"Oh! . . ." fatty quickly covered up, 'I wasn't thinking of *that*."

"Of course not!"

"But we can be engaged. I think my father would like it."

"How romantic. Can't we elope, too?"

Here the loud slamming of the kitchen door ended the little comedy, and who should come steaming into the house but old road-roller, himself. Say, was he ever *mad* after his imprisonment in the barn. Nor was he fooled a single instant by Poppy's disguise.

"So it's *you?*" he thundered, yanking the wig off.

The fat kid's eyes almost popped out of his head.

"Say— Say—" Then his face got red.

"I don't suppose you'll want to keep that date . . . now," purred Poppy, who can take his medicine with a grin.

"I'll punch your head!"

THE GALLOPING SNAIL

"Trickery!" stormed the lawyer. "Base, degrading trickery."

"How about yourself?" Poppy slung back.

"Shut up! And more than that, pack up—the whole caboodle of you—and git out of here."

"That's it, Pa. Kick 'em out. For they threw hornets at me. And water, too."

"They'll suffer for this!"

"Maybe not as much as you think," Poppy stood his ground. "For we've got the goods on you, Mr. Lawyer Chew. A diary that we found here tells how you coaxed Mr. Danver to make a new will. You lied to him, too. He asked you to write to his granddaughter, but you never did. And the law'll fix you for that."

"Silence!"

"Poof!" Poppy snapped his fingers under the fat nose. "You can yell your head off, you big bag of wind, and you can't scare *me*."

"Git out of here!"

"Go for him, Pa. Throw him out."

"Um. . . ." came a drawl from the door, and in swung old Goliath. "Jest try puttin' that boy out, or the tother one, either," says he, rolling up his sleeves, "an' see what happens."

"Who are you?" came the further thunder.

"*Me?*" and the giant posed like an old fool. "I'm jest little Red Riding Hood."

"Are you the man who carried me to the barn?"

"Yep. An' if Poppy says the word, I'll carry you to the front door an' chuck you clean into the road."

Here another voice spoke up.

"Stop!—all of you," cried Mrs. Doane, and the tired, defeated look on the woman's thin white face hurt me like a knife jab. "I've come to the end of my rope." She turned to Chew. "You have won out. I'm sorry. And I shall forever hold it against Corbin Danver for disinheriting his own kin. There were a few things here that I wanted myself," —the poor old soul wiped her eyes—"but I can get along without them. What hurts me worse is Miss Ruth's loss. She asked me to come here, and I did, and I've done everything I could to find her, and to help her. Now, I'm—I'm sick and weary of it all. I'm going to bed. If the rest of you want to go to bed, you'll find plenty of rooms. In the morning I'll pack up my things and go home. . . Good night."

Well, that sort of put an end to the scrap. But I'm not so sure that old Chew wouldn't have dumped us out of the front door, all right, if it hadn't been for Goliath. Yes, the giant saved us . . . and afterwards we remembered it!

Poppy and I felt pretty sick as we crawled into our bed in the big room. It was galling to us to have

THE GALLOPING SNAIL

old Chew win out. Of course, we hadn't lost anything ourselves. But we were on the granddaughter's side. And her loss was our loss, sort of.

Tap! . . . tap! . . . tap! . . .

Jerked out of a crazy dream, I sat up in bed and rubbed my eyes. The gander! It had tapped that way to get into the house. How well I remembered that night! And now it was tapping again. Somewhere in the big room.

Excited, I got Poppy up. And between us we traced the sound to one of the fancy cloth wall panels. As I have written down, these panels were pictures. And in this particular picture there was a big yellow moon.

What was it the diary had said? The hidden staircase behind the moon! There was a secret door here. And if we could open it, the mystery would be over.

Poppy told me then, in a low excited voice, why he had been measuring the room that afternoon. He had suspected that the wall before us was too thick to be natural. Now, in quick measuring, both in the big room and the one next to it, we found that there was a four-foot secret wall chamber here.

And the way to get into that hidden room, where the gander was still tapping, was through the "moon" picture. We felt all over the wall for a hidden spring. Then we pressed the moon itself—and out swung the whole panel!

"Urk! Urk!" says the spotted gander, acting tickled to see us. "Urk! Urk!" and as though to guide us, it turned and started up a flight of winding stairs, flying from step to step.

We followed it, using our flashlight, which showed us that the stairs went down, as well as up. I don't mind telling you that I kept pretty blamed close to the leader. It was a spooky adventure, let me tell you. Where was the gander taking us? What was there up above? Was it a peril of some kind? And surprised by us in its secret den, would it jump at us and try to kill us, as it had tried to kill old Ivory Dome in the barn? You can see what our thoughts were like.

Coming to the top of the stairs, which had taken us almost to the roof, we found ourselves in a little room, which we learned afterwards was a secret part of the big attic. Here we found a cot. And sound asleep on the cot was a *girl*. The prettiest girl I'd ever seen in all my life.

The granddaughter! We had found her hiding place at last! But who could have dreamed that the hiding place was *here?*

CHAPTER XXII

ON THE ROAD AGAIN

WELL, I'm pretty close to the end of my story now. And to sort of hurry things along, I'm not going to write down, word for word, what everybody in the house said and did in the next few hours, for, as you can imagine, there was a lot of tumbling, rambling talk when we took the granddaughter to Mrs. Doane. Instead, I'll go ahead, in my own words, and clear up the mystery for you.

To start with, Dr. Madden wasn't dead at all. He had fainted during his talk with me on the telephone, and that is what had given me the idea that he was gone. I'm glad to say that he got well, and now is in his right mind, which he *wasn't* before the accident, for he had something to tell the medical world that would have been a big loss if the secret had died with him. Can't you guess now why he was hiding in the big house? It was to complete his "cure" for the fatal jungle disease. Experiments had been going on for years, and if the millionaire had lived another twelve months he would have been completely cured. Upon his death, which halted the experiments, Dr. Madden put some of the impure blood into his own body, so that he could go ahead with his work. And, as I say, in the year that he secretly doped himself with drugs, he found a complete cure—he was bright enough on that point, but I guess the *solitude* of the big empty house got the best of him. I don't mean he was crazy—just *queer*.

It was quite by accident that he found the diary. Reading it, to learn if it was his duty, as a friend who knew its probable secrets, to destroy it, he thus had found out about the lawyer's trickery. But instead of writing and telling the granddaughter who he was and *why* she ought to be in the big house when the will was read, he worded his letter so *crazy-like*, with such queer reference to the dead man's diary, that the letter frightened her. She knew all about the big fortune that was waiting to be divided up, and while she had no proof that her grandfather wanted her to have the most of it, still she had been told certain things by Chew, as I'll mention later. And this mysterious, rambling letter, signed by "a friend," urged her to do things that the lawyer had told her not to do. You can see the sort of "up-a-tree" fix that she was in. One man told her to keep away, the other told her to come. And each one hinted that if she didn't do as he said she would cross her grandfather's wishes. So it isn't so strange

THE GALLOPING SNAIL 233

that she made up her mind to come to the big house *secret-like*, where she intended to get the diary and find out the truth. Yet she hadn't the nerve to come to the big house alone. And her mother being in Europe, she got the idea of having two older relatives open up the house for her. Afterwards she would beg their pardon for worrying and mystifying them. And to that point, only the woman was to be left mystified, for it was the girl's intention to take the old man into her confidence.

As we know, the house keys had been sent to her —which was the first she knew that her grandfather was dead—and to his own ends Chew craftily "explained" that she now was the "custodian" of the house, with the duty of seeing that it was kept *completely closed*, the dead man's last wish. It was further hinted that unless she did this she would lose her heritage. Nor did Chew intend to send for her when the will was read. By keeping her away a year, as he had kept her away from the funeral, he would practically get control of everything, and that, of course, is what he was after. Hence the girl took particular pains to caution the two Doanes not to let anybody know that they were living in the big house. How Ma spilled the beans, though, we already know.

On the train the girl got the frightened idea that

a man in "green goggles" was secretly watching her. And when this man followed her from the train in Pardyville, she ran back to her seat, hurriedly writing a note to old Ivory Dome, which note was left with the ticket agent. In leaving home that morning, a boy friend had laughingly given her a pet gander, which he had fixed up in a crazy way with purple ink spots—though what the complete joke was about the gander the girl never told us! I have a hunch, though, that she was kind of sweet on the guy! Anyway, she kept the gander, which was checked to Pardyville. So old Ivory Dome got it, along with the note, when he finally rolled in, twenty minutes late.

The note said that he was to turn back on C. H. O. and keep going until he met the girl on the road, as it was her intention to go to Sandy Ridge, the next stop, and take a taxicab from there. In the meantime, a fence had been put across C. H. O., but old Ivory Dome didn't let that stop him! Whether he went around it, or over it, we don't know. But we do understand now how he happened to have the whole road to himself, and why he passed the sandy crossroad. The concrete having "bulged" dangerously, a mile east of Sandy Ridge, the road had been shut off for temporary repairs. The taxicab brought the girl that far, where old Ivory Dome picked her

THE GALLOPING SNAIL

up. With his promise to keep her secret, she had gotten out of the car before the tip-up. On the east side of the stone house a vine frame cleverly hid a secret door, at the foot of the wall staircase, and going there, while we were fussing over the unconscious man, she found the door *open!* She didn't know, of course, that Dr. Madden was living in the secret room. He had gone outside, at the time of the accident, and later was unable to get back in, for the girl had locked the door on the inside. So now we know why he watched the house that night in the storm.

He tried again the next night to get into the house, but to no success. Later that night he followed us to the barn, after the girl had put the gander in our room to get us away, so that she could clean out the desk in the hope of finding the diary. You will remember, we went into the barn first, then Dr. Madden, then old Ivory Dome. And right here I think I ought to say a few words about the old man. A queer codger, he wasn't half as crafty as we had imagined. It is true that he had promised the granddaughter to keep her secret, but in the automobile accident everything in his thick head had been turned upside-down. His dumbness wasn't put on. *Why* he went to the barn, we'll never know. But I think he remembered, sort of vague-like, that there was a *secret* about the gander, and that may have been why it attracted him. The girl came back to the barn to get the gander, for company, screaming when she saw a "ghost." And the rest you know.

The next morning, before putting old Chew wise to the truth, Poppy went to him with a long face.

"Mr. Chew," says he meekly, "is it possible for you to let bygones be bygones and do me a favor?"

"No, sir!" the old tub thundered, with hatred in his green eyes. "You'll get no favors from me. To the contrary, I'm going to make you sweat for last night's attack. You'll suffer under the law for that."

Poppy was crushed, and showed it.

"I was going to ask you," he hung his head, "if you cared if Mrs. Doane took home the red-plush settee in the hall."

"Mrs. Doane will get *nothing* out of this house."

"Maybe you'll sell it to us, so we can give it to her."

"I wouldn't sell it to you for a thousand dollars," came meanly, "if I knew she wanted it."

Some old hog, huh? Well, I'm glad to write down in conclusion that the good old lady *did* get her settee —with ten thousand dollars on top of it—and all fatty got, after all of his crooked work, was what the little boy shot at. Which is the way things should be.

To show you how much "brotherly love" he had

THE GALLOPING SNAIL 237

for the New Zion bunch, he practically put them out of business by making them pay fourteen per cent on money that they owed the Danver estate. The estate got five per cent and old grab-it-all got the rest!

And thus reminded of old Goliath, you'll give us the horselaugh when I tell you the truth about *him*. He wasn't married at all. Furthermore, he was the only man left in the religious camp—he was so hard-boiled and such a liar that the others, in moving away, wouldn't even take him with them, though earlier they had tried to use him and reform him. No wonder the "town" had looked deserted the day we rode through it in state—after having coughed up two dollars for the privilege! The houses had been empty for six months. And we had swallowed that "picnic" story! Old Goliath sure worked us slick. I suppose he's laughing about it to this day. Well, we should worry. We still have his hair!

The balance of our hitch-hike was kind of tame. So we were glad to get home. And to that point, we hadn't been home a week before we were mixed up in the Pedigreed-Pickle business that the Tutter people are still laughing over. Can you imagine Poppy standing up to his neck in cucumber pickles? It was his job to sell the pickles—but before he could *sell* them he had to *make* them. I can still see that mountain of cucumbers. "It's no use," says I, in despair. "We can't do it."

But we did. And *how* we did it—bucked by a mean rich kid, and with a mystery hanging over us that gave us shivers one minute and completely tangled us up the next—is, I believe, a story that you won't want to miss.

So tighten up your buttons for the biggest laugh of your lifetime, for we'll soon be there in POPPY OTT'S PEDIGREED PICKLES.

—THE END—

This Isn't All!

Would you like to know what became of the good friends you have made in this book?

Would you like to read other stories continuing their adventures and experiences, or other books quite as entertaining by the same author?

On the *reverse side* of the wrapper which comes with this book, you will find a wonderful list of stories which you can buy at the same store where you got this book.

Don't throw away the Wrapper

Use it as a handy catalog of the books you want some day to have. But in case you do mislay it, write to the Publishers for a complete catalog.

BOOKS BY LEO EDWARDS

Illustrated. Individual Colored Wrappers. Every Volume Complete in Itself.

Hundreds of thousands of boys who laughed until their sides ached over the weird and wonderful adventures of Jerry Todd and his gang demanded that Leo Edwards, the author, give them more books with belt-bursting laughs and creepy shivers. So he took Poppy Ott, Jerry Todd's bosom chum and created the Poppy Ott series. Now there are two more series, The Andy Blake and the Trigger Berg—and if such a thing is possible—they are even more full of fun and excitement than the Jerry Todds.

THE JERRY TODD BOOKS

JERRY TODD AND THE WHISPERING MUMMY
JERRY TODD AND THE ROSE COLORED CAT
JERRY TODD AND THE OAK ISLAND TREASURE
JERRY TODD AND THE WALTZING HEN
JERRY TODD AND THE TALKING FROG
JERRY TODD AND THE PURRING EGG
JERRY TODD IN THE WHISPERING CAVE
JERRY TODD, PIRATE
JERRY TODD AND THE BOB-TAILED ELEPHANT

THE POPPY OTT BOOKS

POPPY OTT AND THE STUTTERING PARROT
POPPY OTT AND THE SEVEN LEAGUE STILTS
POPPY OTT AND THE GALLOPING SNAIL
POPPY OTT'S PEDIGREED PICKLES
POPPY OTT AND THE FRECKLED GOLDFISH
POPPY OTT AND THE TITTERING TOTEM

THE ANDY BLAKE BOOKS

ANDY BLAKE
ANDY BLAKE'S COMET COASTER
ANDY BLAKE'S SECRET SERVICE

THE TRIGGER BERG BOOKS

TRIGGER BERG AND THE TREASURE TREE
TRIGGER BERG AND THE 700 MOUSETRAPS

GROSSET & DUNLAP, Publishers, NEW YORK

BUDDY BOOKS FOR BOYS

Illustrated. Individual Colored Wrappers

Tales of old Western pioneer days and the California gold fields, tales of mystery, humor, adventure, thrilling stories of sports and aviation. There is a wide range of subjects in this list of titles—all by well known authors of books for boys.

BEAN BALL BILL............................William Heyliger
    A book filled with adventure and sport by a favorite boys' author.

MARK GILMORE, SCOUT OF THE AIR...Percy Keese Fitzhugh
    The story of how a boy scout falls in with an aviator and helps him accomplish a mission.

CAMERON MACBAIN, BACKWOODSMAN.Harold M. Sherman
    A boy from the backwoods has some strange adventures in the city.

FLYING HEELS............................Harold M. Sherman
    How a postponed hockey game brought about a thrilling series of events.

FLASHING STEEL.........................Harold M. Sherman
    A great hockey story which tells of a game between an American championship team and a Canadian championship team.

BUFFALO BOY..................................J. Allan Dunn
    A boy's adventure in the old pioneer days.

THE CLOUD PATROL..........................Irving Crump
    The thrilling experiences of a young air pilot.

THE PILOT OF THE CLOUD PATROL.........Irving Crump
    A sequel to "The Cloud Patrol."

DON RAIDER, TRAIL BLAZER............Harold M. Sherman
    Don was not used to the city but he knew how to handle himself against an alley gang that was set against him.

TUCK SIMMS, FORTY NINER...............Edward Leonard
    Excitement and danger in the California gold fields.

WIGWAG WEIGAND......................Percy Keese Fitzhugh
    A charming story of mystery and true fellowship.

HERVEY WILLETTS.....................Percy Keese Fitzhugh
    Readers of Tom Slade and Roy Blakeley will be glad to learn more of Hervey Willetts.

SKINNY McCORD........................Percy Keese Fitzhugh
    Skinny is a queer, amusing chap and he has a lot of thrilling adventures.

GROSSET & DUNLAP, *Publishers,* NEW YORK

FLYING STORIES FOR BOYS

IN THE AIR WITH ANDY LANE
By EUSTACE L. ADAMS

**Individual Colored Wrappers. Illustrated.
Every Volume Complete in Itself.**

May be had wherever books are sold. Ask for Grosset & Dunlap's list

Mr. Adams, the author of this flying series for boys is an experienced aviator and has had many thrilling adventures in the air—both as a member of the famous Lafayette Escadrille in the World War and in the United States Naval Aviation Service flying with the squadrons patrolling the Atlantic Coast. His stories reveal not only his ability to tell daring and exciting air episodes but also his first hand knowledge of modern aeroplanes and the marvelous technical improvements which have been made in the past few years. Andy Lane flies the latest and most highly developed machines in the field of aviation.

FIFTEEN DAYS IN THE AIR
Andy refuels his ship in the air and sets a new endurance record.

OVER THE POLAR ICE
In a giant flying boat Andy beats his enemy in a dash to the South Pole.

RACING ROUND THE WORLD
In a series of thrilling flights Andy wins an air dash around the globe to win a $100,000 prize.

THE RUNAWAY AIRSHIP
Through foggy skies Andy Lane brings back the world's greatest passenger carrying dirigible, blown away on the wings of a storm.

PIRATES OF THE AIR
Andy Lane pilots the giant passenger plane Apex No. 4 across the Atlantic in the face of almost overwhelming odds.

ON THE WINGS OF FLAME
Andy makes a forced landing in the South American jungle in the dead of night and has thrilling experiences with the natives.

GROSSET & DUNLAP, Publishers, NEW YORK

THE REX LEE FLYING STORIES
By THOMSON BURTIS

Individual Colored Wrappers. Illustrated. Every Volume Complete in Itself.

May be had wherever books are sold. Ask for Grosset & Dunlap's list.

The author of this series of exciting flying stories is an experienced aviator. He says, "During my five years in the army I performed nearly every sort of flying duty—instructor, test pilot, bombing, photographing pilot, etc., in every variety of ship, from tiny scout planes to the gigantic three-motored Italian Caproni."

Not only has this author had many experiences as a flyer; a list of his activities while knocking around the country includes postal clerk, hobo, actor, writer, mutton chop salesman, preacher, roughneck in the oil fields, newspaper man, flyer, scenario writer in Hollywood and synthetic clown with the Sells Floto Circus. Having lived an active, daring life, and possessing a gift for good story telling, he is well qualified to write these adventures of a red-blooded dare devil young American who became one of the country's greatest flyers.

REX LEE; GYPSY FLIER
REX LEE; ON THE BORDER PATROL
REX LEE; RANGER OF THE SKY
REX LEE; SKY TRAILER
REX LEE; ACE OF THE AIR MAIL
REX LEE; NIGHT FLIER
REX LEE'S MYSTERIOUS FLIGHT

GROSSET & DUNLAP, Publishers, NEW YORK

THE TOM SLADE BOOKS
By PERCY KEESE FITZHUGH
Author of "Roy Blakeley," "Pee-wee Harris," "Westy Martin," Etc.

Illustrated. Individual Picture Wrappers in Colors. Every Volume Complete in Itself.

"Let your boy grow up with Tom Slade," is a suggestion which thousands of parents have followed during the past, with the result that the TOM SLADE BOOKS are the most popular boys' books published today. They take Tom Slade through a series of typical boy adventures through his tenderfoot days as a scout, through his gallant days as an American doughboy in France, back to his old patrol and the old camp ground at Black Lake, and so on.

TOM SLADE, BOY SCOUT
TOM SLADE AT TEMPLE CAMP
TOM SLADE ON THE RIVER
TOM SLADE WITH THE COLORS
TOM SLADE ON A TRANSPORT
TOM SLADE WITH THE BOYS OVER THERE
TOM SLADE MOTORCYCLE DISPATCH BEARER
TOM SLADE WITH THE FLYING CORPS
TOM SLADE AT BLACK LAKE
TOM SLADE ON MYSTERY TRAIL
TOM SLADE'S DOUBLE DARE
TOM SLADE ON OVERLOOK MOUNTAIN
TOM SLADE PICKS A WINNER
TOM SLADE AT BEAR MOUNTAIN
TOM SLADE: FOREST RANGER
TOM SLADE IN THE NORTH WOODS
TOM SLADE AT SHADOW ISLE
TOM SLADE IN THE HAUNTED CAVERN

GROSSET & DUNLAP, *Publishers,* **NEW YORK**

THE ROY BLAKELEY BOOKS
By PERCY KEESE FITZHUGH
Author of "Tom Slade," "Pee-wee Harris," "Westy Martin," Etc.

**Illustrated. Picture Wrappers in Color.
Every Volume Complete in Itself.**

In the character and adventures of Roy Blakeley are typified the very essence of Boy life. He is a real boy, as real as Huck Finn and Tom Sawyer. He is the moving spirit of the troop of Scouts of which he is a member, and the average boy has to go only a little way in the first book before Roy is the best friend he ever had, and he is willing to part with his best treasure to get the next book in the series.

ROY BLAKELEY
ROY BLAKELEY'S ADVENTURES IN CAMP
ROY BLAKELEY, PATHFINDER
ROY BLAKELEY'S CAMP ON WHEELS
ROY BLAKELEY'S SILVER FOX PATROL
ROY BLAKELEY'S MOTOR CARAVAN
ROY BLAKELEY, LOST, STRAYED OR STOLEN
ROY BLAKELEY'S BEE-LINE HIKE
ROY BLAKELEY AT THE HAUNTED CAMP
ROY BLAKELEY'S FUNNY BONE HIKE
ROY BLAKELEY'S TANGLED TRAIL
ROY BLAKELEY ON THE MOHAWK TRAIL
ROY BLAKELEY'S ELASTIC HIKE
ROY BLAKELEY'S ROUNDABOUT HIKE
ROY BLAKELEY'S HAPPY-GO-LUCKY HIKE
ROY BLAKELEY'S GO-AS YOU PLEASE HIKE
ROY BLAKELEY'S WILD GOOSE CHASE

GROSSET & DUNLAP, *Publishers*, NEW YORK

Football and Baseball Stories

**Durably Bound. Illustrated. Colored Wrappers
Every Volume Complete in Itself.**

The Ralph Henry Barbour Books For Boys

In these up-to the minute, spirited genuine stories of boy life there is something which will appeal to every boy with the love of manliness, cleanness and sportsmanship in his heart.

LEFT END EDWARDS
LEFT TACKLE THAYER
LEFT GUARD GILBERT
CENTER RUSH ROWLAND
FULLBACK FOSTER
LEFT HALF HARMON
RIGHT END EMERSON
RIGHT GUARD GRANT
QUARTERBACK BATES
RIGHT TACKLE TODD
RIGHT HALF HOLLINS

The Tod Hale Series

TOD HALE IN CAMP
TOD HALE WITH THE CREW
TOD HALE ON THE SCRUB

The Christy Mathewson Books For Boys

Every boy wants to know how to play ball in the fairest and squarest way. These books about boys and baseball are full of wholesome and manly interest and information.

PITCHER POLLOCK
CATCHER CRAIG
FIRST BASE FAULKNER
SECOND BASE SLOAN
PITCHING IN A PINCH

THIRD BASE THATCHER, By Everett Scott.

GROSSET & DUNLAP, PUBLISHERS, NEW YORK

THE PEE-WEE HARRIS BOOKS
By PERCY KEESE FITZHUGH
Author of "Tom Slade," "Roy Blakeley," "Westy Martin," Etc.

Illustrated. Individual Picture Wrappers in Color. Every Volume Complete in Itself.

All readers of the Tom Slade and the Roy Blakeley books are acquainted with Pee-wee Harris. These stories record the true facts concerning his size (what there is of it) and his heroism (such as it is), his voice, his clothes, his appetite, his friends, his enemies, his victims. Together with the thrilling narrative of how he foiled, baffled, circumvented and triumphed over everything and everybody (except where he failed) and how even when he failed he succeeded. The whole recorded in a series of screams and told with neither muffler nor cut-out.

PEE-WEE HARRIS
PEE-WEE HARRIS ON THE TRAIL
PEE-WEE HARRIS IN CAMP
PEE-WEE HARRIS IN LUCK
PEE-WEE HARRIS ADRIFT
PEE-WEE HARRIS F. O. B. BRIDGEBORO
PEE-WEE HARRIS FIXER
PEE-WEE HARRIS: AS GOOD AS HIS WORD
PEE-WEE HARRIS: MAYOR FOR A DAY
PEE-WEE HARRIS AND THE SUNKEN TREASURE
PEE-WEE HARRIS ON THE BRINY DEEP
PEE-WEE HARRIS IN DARKEST AFRICA

GROSSET & DUNLAP, *Publishers,* NEW YORK

THE WESTY MARTIN BOOKS
By PERCY KEESE FITZHUGH
Author of the "Tom Slade" and "Roy Blakeley"
Books, Etc.

**Individual Colored Wrappers. Illustrated.
Every Volume Complete in Itself.**

May be had wherever books are sold. Ask for Grosset & Dunlap's list

Westy Martin, known to every friend of Roy Blakeley, appears as the hero of adventures quite different from those in which we have seen him participate as a Scout of Bridgeboro and Temple Camp. On his way to the Yellowstone the bigness of the vast West and the thoughts of the wild preserve that he is going to visit make him conscious of his own smallness and the futility of "boy scouting" and woods lore in this great region. Yet he was to learn that if it had not been for his scout training he would never have been able to survive the experiences he had in these stories.

WESTY MARTIN

WESTY MARTIN IN THE YELLOWSTONE

WESTY MARTIN IN THE ROCKIES

WESTY MARTIN ON THE SANTE FE TRAIL

WESTY MARTIN ON THE OLD INDIAN TRAIL

WESTY MARTIN IN THE LAND OF THE PURPLE SAGE

GROSSET & DUNLAP, Publishers, NEW YORK